CABIN FEVER

"I'm going to deliver my piece of this deal," the man said to Frank and Joe, "collect my reward, and sail off into the sunset. I'll live happily ever after in Brazil or maybe Argentina—someplace where they know how to treat a man with money and aren't likely to send me back to the U.S. After all, it may get a little hot around here pretty soon."

He shook the pack of matches and with a long, mournful sigh slowly opened the door of the cabin.

"It's been nice knowin' you fellas. Sorry it had to end like this." He stepped through the door and slammed it shut behind him.

Frank glanced over at Joe, whose skin had gone ash gray. Frank knew he was probably the same color himself. He yanked frantically on his bonds, but they didn't give at all. And then he smelled it.

"Smoke!" Frank said, feeling the panic rising inside him. "Joe—he's s

Books in THE HARDY BOYS CASEFILES™ Series

Available from ARCHWAY Paperbacks

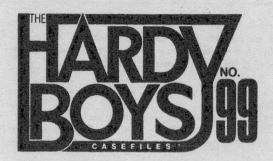

THE HARDY BOYS CASEFILES NO. 99

FRAME-UP

FRANKLIN W. DIXON

AN ARCHWAY PAPERBACK
Published by POCKET BOOKS
New York   London   Toronto   Sydney   Tokyo   Singapore

This book is a work of fiction. Names, characters, places and incidents are products of the author's imagination or are used fictitiously. Any resemblance to actual events or locales or persons, living or dead, is entirely coincidental.

AN ARCHWAY PAPERBACK *Original*

An Archway Paperback published by
POCKET BOOKS, a division of Simon & Schuster Inc.
1230 Avenue of the Americas, New York, NY 10020

Copyright © 1995 by Simon & Schuster Inc.
Produced by Mega-Books, Inc.

ISBN: 0-671-88210-4

First Archway Paperback printing May 1995

10 9 8 7 6 5 4 3 2 1

THE HARDY BOYS, AN ARCHWAY PAPERBACK and colophon are registered trademarks of Simon & Schuster Inc.

THE HARDY BOYS CASEFILES is a trademark of Simon & Schuster Inc.

Cover art by Brian Kotzky

Printed in the U.S.A.

IL 6+

FRAME-UP

Chapter

1

"THIS IS AWESOME," Joe Hardy said to his brother, Frank, as they stood gazing up at the huge, vaulted glass and steel ceiling of the New Orleans Convention Center.

"I know what you mean," Frank said with a smile, running a hand through his dark brown hair. "I feel like we're in some cyborg city in the twenty-fifth century."

The two brothers were surrounded by hundreds of people swarming around the floor, eagerly checking out Computer Horizons, a technology trade show featuring the latest in software, hardware, robotics, and computer peripherals. The Hardys moved along with the crowd until they found themselves in front of a display with remote cameras guided by a central terminal. The terminal had several high-resolution color monitors that were being watched by a human-looking robot.

"These computerized security systems are incredible," Frank commented.

The boys' father, Fenton Hardy, was a well-known private investigator back in Bayport. When Joe's girlfriend, Vanessa Bender, had announced that she was flying down to New Orleans to check out software for her mother's graphics business, Mr. Hardy had sent Frank and Joe along, too. Their assignment was to investigate the latest in security systems technology.

"But there's too much to see," Joe went on. "I mean, we've been in New Orleans all day and haven't taken one step outside the convention center."

"Then why don't you round up Vanessa and we'll hit the road," Frank replied.

"She said she'd meet us in the lobby at six o'clock," Joe replied.

"That gives us exactly five minutes," Frank said, checking his watch. "Let's go!"

The boys made it to their meeting place on time, but it was a quarter of an hour before Joe spied Vanessa riding down the escalator. She was standing next to a dark-haired guy who looked as if he'd just stepped out of a men's fashion magazine. He wore a finely tailored European-cut suit, and his dark, deep-set eyes were fixed on Vanessa. At the bottom of the escalator, Vanessa flashed the guy a brilliant smile and led him over to meet the Hardys.

"Hi, you two!" she said. "Isn't this show the most fantastic thing you've ever seen?"

"Yeah," Joe grunted. "Fantastic."

"Joe, Frank—I'd like you to meet Billy Barta. Billy—Frank and Joe Hardy, the guys I came down here with."

"Pleased to meet you," Barta said politely, with a faint accent that Joe couldn't place.

"Hi." Joe shook Billy's hand, although he didn't much like the guy.

"What's the matter, Joe?" Vanessa asked him. "You sound unhappy."

"Me?" Joe said. "No, I'm okay. Just tired."

"We've been on our feet all day," Frank explained.

"I understand," Billy said, smiling slightly. "Well, nice meeting y'all. Vanessa, see you around sometime, eh?" With that, he departed. Joe noticed that Vanessa stared at him as he walked away.

"Well," Frank said to Vanessa, "we're hungry, thirsty, and ready to party."

"Sounds good to me," Vanessa replied with a happy shrug. "And you'll be glad to know, I've got it all arranged. We're going to Tipitina's—it's a gigantic club in the French Quarter. Ultimate

Graphics Software is throwing a bash there at eight, and since I bought some of their programs for my mom, I got us all an invitation! I called Catlin, and she's coming, too. So let's go get our luggage out of the lockers and head for our home away from home."

Catlin was an old friend of Vanessa's. She lived in New Orleans with her aunt Violet. Frank, Joe, and Vanessa were going to stay at Violet's house for the entire five days they were in town.

"So, Vanessa," Joe broke in as they headed to the wall of lockers behind the escalators. "Who's your new friend?"

"New friend?" Vanessa asked, puzzled. "You mean Billy? He was looking at software beside me, and we just got talking."

"What about?" Joe asked casually.

"About software, actually. Billy is here to check out inventory control systems for his boss's company. He's incredibly knowledgeable. And his boss, Ron Stolarz, has a big warehouse down on the docks—"

"Fascinating," Joe said as he pulled their luggage out of the lockers.

"And besides storing the stuff he imports and exports," Vanessa went on, "Billy's boss also uses his warehouse as a place to build floats for Mardi Gras."

"Wait a minute," Frank said. "You mean if we

went down there, we could see one getting built?"

"Probably not at this time of year," Vanessa said, grabbing her backpack. "But he stores a lot of the old ones there, so we could check them out."

"Maybe we'd better pass on it," Frank said warily. "Joe's jealous enough of this Billy as it is."

"Jealous? Me?" Joe asked in disbelief. "No way!"

"Uh-huh," Vanessa said, linking her arm with Joe's and leading the Hardy brothers out of the building. "Then you might be interested in the fact that he's part Cajun. Pretty exotic, huh? He's got the cutest accent—"

"Enough, okay?" Joe pleaded. "Let's just get out of here. I can't wait to eat. What's good around here?"

"How about blackened redfish or some gumbo, Joe?" Frank suggested. "You'll feel much better after you've had some."

They found their rental car, a red convertible, at the far end of the lot where they'd parked it that morning, then headed down St. Charles with Frank at the wheel. Old iron streetcars clattered past them, running along the tracks on the Esplanade in the middle of the street. Soon they arrived in the Garden District, where Catlin and her aunt Violet lived.

The house they were looking for was on Calumet, a quiet street off St. Charles. It had turrets, a wraparound porch, magnolia trees in front, and was painted light gray with pink and white trim. "Whoa," Joe said. "Nice place! Is this where we're staying?"

"It's been in Catlin's family for generations," Vanessa told him. "Her aunt Violet's lived here all her life. She's never married, but Catlin tells me she's married to her work—running major community projects. Oh, look. There's Cat!"

Catlin was sitting on the porch waiting for them. She had straight, shoulder-length blond hair, large green eyes, and a mischievous smile.

"Hey, y'all!" she called out, waving to them as Frank pulled the convertible into the long gravel driveway.

"Catlin!" Vanessa shouted, rushing over to embrace her friend as Frank and Joe followed close behind.

"Welcome to Big Easy, kids!" Catlin greeted them. "Havin' a good time so far?"

"Getting better every minute," Frank said, giving her a warm smile.

"You must be Frank," Catlin said, extending her hand for him to shake. " 'Cause I know Joe's the blond."

"You got it right," Frank said, shaking hands with her.

"Well, what are we waitin' for?" Catlin asked.

"Y'all come on in and get changed, so we can go partyin'!"

"Where's your aunt?" Vanessa asked.

"Oh, she's off at some meeting. I think this state couldn't get along without Aunt Vi. Her energy could power the whole of Louisiana."

Frank was amazed at the number of mementos and knickknacks Catlin's aunt had managed to cram into one house. Yet the place was cozy and welcoming. "This is great," he said as Catlin led them upstairs to their rooms.

"Glad you like it," Catlin said. "Here's your room, fellas. Meet y'all downstairs in fifteen minutes. There'll be food at Tipitina's, but the party's not till eight. If you're starving, I know a great little place in the Quarter."

"I'm starving," Frank replied, shutting the door behind the girls. Then he turned to Joe and said, "You know, I think I'm going to like it here."

"Now, this is more like it!" Joe said, patting his full stomach as the four of them sauntered down the narrow, gaslit streets of the French Quarter after dinner.

Houses with arched doorways and ironwork balconies surrounded them as they walked down Bourbon Street. The warm air was perfumed with the scent of oleander and hibiscus, music poured out of the doorways of clubs, and neon lights flashed invitingly.

"Glad to see your mood's improved," Frank said, putting an arm around his brother's shoulder. "I knew that all you needed was a good dinner."

"There's Tipitina's," Catlin said, pointing to a large white building with a red neon sign. "Come on!"

Entering the club, they were greeted by a blast of music, the smell of frying shrimp. The place was pulsating with colored spotlights, flashing electric signs, and dancing bodies. A long table with a hot and cold buffet stood at one end of the room, a dance floor at the other.

"Let's dance," Catlin said to Frank, and the two of them disappeared into the mass of people on the floor.

Joe and Vanessa followed.

A solid hour later while they were still dancing, someone tapped Joe lightly on the shoulder. Turning, he saw the smiling face of Billy Barta. "Howdy," he said. "Mind if I cut in?"

Joe wanted to tell the guy to get lost, but he noticed that Vanessa didn't act disappointed to see him. He simply shrugged and walked over to the buffet table where Frank and Catlin were sipping cold lemonade.

"That Barta guy is here," Joe told them, grabbing a lemonade from the table and downing it. He wiped off his mouth and looked back at the floor. Vanessa seemed to enjoy dancing with the guy. Had she known he was planning to come? Joe wondered.

"Probably just a coincidence," Frank ventured, reading his younger brother's mind.

When the music ended, Joe walked back out onto the dance floor and reached for Vanessa's hand.

Billy Barta smoothly stepped between them, though. "How about one more, Vanessa?" he asked.

"Well, I don't know—" Vanessa began. She looked from Billy to Joe, and back to Billy again.

"Ah, come on," Barta said. "You two have your whole lives to dance together."

Vanessa took a step backward, but Billy moved toward her. "I just want my buddies to see me dancin' with the most gorgeous girl on the floor," he pleaded.

Vanessa dropped her head and smiled. It was obvious to Joe that Billy's smooth way of handing out compliments was getting to her.

"That looks like a yes to me," Barta said. When Joe didn't speak up right away, he swept Vanessa into his arms and danced away.

When Joe got back to the buffet table, Frank commented, "Your fists are clenched."

All through the dance—which was a slow number—Vanessa kept glancing over at Joe to make sure he was all right. Still, whenever she looked at Billy Barta, her eyes lit up. When the number ended, Joe started toward them.

"One more!" Billy Barta shouted to the band, and they struck up another number. Billy spun Vanessa around as Joe stood there, stunned and furious.

"Easy, Joe," Frank said, coming up behind him and putting a restraining hand on his arm.

Joe had had about all he could take and strode forward. He put a hand on Barta's arm. "You said 'one more' last time," he pointed out.

"Aw, come on," Barta said, smiling. "Be a sport."

"She's my girl, pal," Joe said hotly, pulling Billy's hand off Vanessa's arm. "So move off!"

Barta's answer was a shove that sent Joe staggering backward into a cement pillar.

"Hey!" Joe said. "Nobody pushes me around!" He raised his fists, ready for action.

"No!" Vanessa screamed. "Joe, stop!"

Joe paid no attention as he headed for Billy Barta with murder in his eyes.

Chapter

2

Joe was quick, but fortunately Frank was quicker. In a split second he had his younger brother in a tight hold. "Take it easy, Joe!" he said.

"Let me at him!" Joe yelled.

Billy Barta stepped back. "Hey, what'd I do?" he asked the onlookers.

Meanwhile Frank pulled Joe toward the front of the club. Tipitina's bouncer held the door open for the brothers, then slammed it hard after them.

"Why'd you do that?" Joe asked hotly as he straightened his shirt.

"Someday you'll thank me for it," Frank said.

"Yeah, right," Joe grumbled. Then he turned to Vanessa, who, along with Catlin, had followed the brothers outside. "What were you doing?" he asked her.

Vanessa stared at him blankly, her face glowing red in the light of Tipitina's neon sign. "Dancing!" she said incredulously. "You didn't have to get all hot and bothered about it. Grow up. You're not my boss!"

Joe stood silently thinking, then said, "Sorry. I did act like an idiot. I'll work on it."

"What? Acting like an idiot? I don't think you need any more practice." Vanessa finally accepted his apology and hooked her arm through his as they made their way to the car.

On Sunday morning Frank and Joe awoke to the ringing of dozens of church bells. Catlin's aunt Violet greeted the brothers as they came downstairs. One glance at the fiftyish woman told Joe that Aunt Violet at Catlin's age must once have been as gorgeous as her niece. She, too, had large, wide-set green eyes and regular features. Her hair, which she wore in a ponytail, was streaked with gray. She was vibrant, slender, and athletic—in fact, everything about Violet Ribodeaux pulsed with energy, from her bright smile to her faded blue jeans and tennis sneakers.

"You must be Frank and Joe," she said, graciously extending a hand to each of them in turn. "Breakfast's in the dining room. The girls are already eatin'. By the way, Catlin tells me you boys almost got in a fight last night." She gazed at them with almost unbearable directness.

"It's true, I'm afraid," Joe said apologetically.

"Mmmm," Violet said, frowning her disapproval. Then all at once she added, "Well, come along, you two." She led them into the dining room, where Vanessa and Catlin were sitting at the long mahogany table.

Aunt Violet went over to the sideboard and returned with a tray full of pastry rolls and coffee cups. "Café au lait and beignets," she announced. "Best cure for wounded pride I know. Here, Joe—take two."

"I think I will," Joe said, reaching for a roll and a cup.

"What did you say these rolls were called?" Frank asked, biting into one. "They're awesome!"

"Beignets," Violet said. "Come on and eat up, y'all. The convention center's already open, and it's the last day. Besides, I've got a community board meeting to go to."

"You won't believe the stuff they've got at the computer show, Cat," Vanessa said excitedly.

"Oh, computers an' me don't get along," Catlin said.

"Wait till you see these," Frank told her. "They're incredibly user-friendly. You might surprise yourself."

*　　*　　*

Sure enough, Catlin was totally awed by the incredible displays at the convention center. The floor was covered with the best that the international computer companies could muster—flight simulators for everything from airliners to fighter planes, virtual reality equipment, robots, industrial controls, even a spooky military camera that could pick one person out of a crowd and track him as long as he was in sight.

"The freebies are the best part!" Vanessa exclaimed, as she grabbed a Computer Horizons baseball cap.

There were all kinds of handouts—everything from disks loaded with game software, to T-shirts emblazoned with the logos of various companies, to a sleek-looking flashlight that hooked onto a belt loop.

"Vanessa, how are you going to hold all that stuff?" Joe asked her.

"No problem," Vanessa assured him, striding over to a nearby display table. "Excuse me, sir, are these backpacks free samples?"

"Yes," said the burly exhibitor. "But only one per customer."

"Thanks!" Vanessa grabbed one, and brought it over to her friends. "Check this out, guys!" she exclaimed. "We can stuff all our goodies in here—but the backpack is mine."

As they proceeded to lighten their loads, a

voice rang out from across the showing floor. Joe stiffened as he saw Billy Barta waving at them.

"Hey, y'all!" he called, coming their way. "Long time, no see." He, too, sported a black backpack like Vanessa's.

Joe couldn't believe the nerve of this guy! But the handsome man didn't seem at all fazed by what had happened the night before.

"Hey, Joe—no hard feelin's about last night, eh? Sorry if I got a little pushy. I didn't mean anythin' by it."

Joe took the hand Billy offered him and nodded solemnly. He knew he ought to say something, but somehow the words stuck in his throat.

"Hey, how about a bite o' lunch on me?" Billy offered. "It's the least I can do. And they make a real good po' boy sandwich in the café at the other end of the floor."

Joe and the others exchanged glances. "Why not?" he asked, shrugging. "It's about that time."

"See that display over there?" Billy asked as they walked down the exhibit floor. He pointed to an array of cameras and monitors, all controlled by a large bank of computers. "That's the system my boss, Ron Stolarz, sent me down here to check out. He keeps some very valuable merchandise in his warehouses and wants to know exactly where it is at all times."

Barta led them to a table by the snack bar.

"Here we go," he said. "What'll y'all have? Po' boys?"

They ate the delicious sandwiches quickly, and then Billy stood up to excuse himself. "Got to go," he announced. "Bad thing about having this convention in my hometown is that I can still get a little work done. I'm goin' to head over to my place in the Quarter to make a few business calls."

"Your place?" Frank asked, surprised. "Don't you work at the warehouse?"

"It's my own *private* business," Billy said with a knowing wink. "Old Stolarz doesn't have to know everything, eh?"

He slapped Frank on the back. "Maybe I'll see y'all at one of the parties tonight," he added. "If not, well, it's been nice knowing you—'specially the pretty lady here," he said pointedly, taking Vanessa's hand and kissing it. "Sorry, Joe—couldn't resist." He gave Joe a wink, picked up his black backpack, and walked off.

"Quite a guy," Frank said, shaking his head.

"I think he's gorgeous," Catlin ventured. "Did he give you his number, Van?"

"He said it was listed," Vanessa said. "But if you're going to call him, wait till we're out of town, okay?"

"Well, let's get back out onto the floor," Frank said. "We don't want to miss a thing, right, Vanessa?"

"Right!"

Since Vanessa had already settled on the graphics software for her mother's business, she and Catlin went off to watch a virtual reality demonstration. Meanwhile, the Hardys checked out more of the ultra-sophisticated security systems their dad had sent them down to investigate. The best one featured heat and motion sensors, tied directly into a passive alarm system connected to the local police station.

Later, when they all met again in the lobby, Vanessa asked them what they'd thought of the last system they'd seen.

"I'll tell you one thing," Frank answered, "if I were a criminal and I ran into one of them, I'd take off."

"It was a bit much for Bayport, if you ask me," Joe said. "More suited to the kind of sophisticated crime rings you find in a big city, like New York or L.A."

"Or New Orleans?" Catlin put in.

"New Orleans?" Frank repeated in mock astonishment. "Do they have crime here? I'm shocked!"

"Yeah, we've been here for a day and a half and haven't run into a crime yet!" Joe added.

"What the guys mean," Vanessa explained, "is that they seem to attract trouble wherever they go."

"Well, do me a favor," Catlin said. "Let's just

have a good time, and leave the trouble for when you go home."

"You've got a deal," Joe said happily.

"Hey," Vanessa said, checking her watch. "It's almost five. Did you guys want to check out the MicroJet party tonight? 'Cause I'd love to go back to the house, take a shower, and change first."

"Good idea," Joe said. "Here, Vanessa, let me carry the bag. It's my turn. It must be really heavy, with all the stuff we've crammed into it."

"Not at all," Vanessa protested.

"Hey, you're right!" Joe said, surprised at how light the bag felt. "Uh-oh. Wait a minute—" He zipped open the backpack and confirmed his suspicion. "Bad news, you guys. Billy Barta walked off with Vanessa's backpack. This one's his, see? There's practically nothing in it."

"Oh, no!" Vanessa moaned. "Are we going to have to go back and start collecting all over again? It'll take hours!"

"Wait," Frank said. "I've got a better idea— you said Billy Barta's phone number was listed, right?"

"Yeah," Vanessa said.

"Give him a ring," Frank suggested. "He said he lived in the Quarter. Maybe we could go over and get your bag back."

"Great idea!" Vanessa said. She went to a phone booth, but was back moments later. "No one was home," she said. "Didn't he say he was going back there to make some calls?"

"Maybe he changed his mind or got done already," Joe said. "That was a few hours ago."

"We could try again later, on our way to the party," Frank suggested. "It's in the Quarter, too."

After showering and changing at Aunt Violet's, they tried Billy's number again. Still no answer. Vanessa wrote down his address, which was also listed in the phone book. "He lives over on Chartres Street," she said. "That's only a few blocks from the party."

"Great!" Joe said. "I'll go over to Billy's myself while you guys party."

"Oh, Joe, you don't need to do that," Vanessa protested.

"No, it should be me," Joe insisted. "I want to show the guy I'm not holding any grudges, you know?"

With their plans formed, the foursome headed back downtown. Joe said goodbye to the others outside the club and walked over to Chartres Street, where he found Billy's address.

The house was a run-down two-story affair in the most touristy part of the Quarter. Billy's address, 241 ½, was around at the rear of the building. Joe opened the ironwork gate and headed back there, walking under a brick archway, away from the streetlights. Joe felt as if invisible eyes were watching him. "Ridiculous," he said to himself, shaking his head to rid the feeling that something was wrong.

From inside Billy's apartment loud jazz music was playing, yet the door hung carelessly open. Somebody's going to break in here one of these days, if he isn't more careful, Joe thought as he knocked.

No one answered. Joe figured that Billy couldn't hear him because the music was turned up so loud, so he opened the door the rest of the way and stuck his head through.

"Billy?" he called out loudly.

Then Joe saw him. Billy Barta lay sprawled on the floor, the hair on the back of his head matted with blood!

Joe froze for a moment. Then he moved quickly and purposefully. A brief examination of the body showed that Billy had been hit with a blunt instrument. Joe felt for a pulse. There was none, but the body was still warm. Joe figured he'd been murdered within the last few minutes. He glanced nervously around the room, realizing that the killer might still be around.

Soundlessly, Joe got up and tiptoed to the bedroom door. Luckily, there was no one there, or anywhere else in Billy's messy, cluttered apartment. Joe shut off the loud music, but made sure not to disturb anything else. His brief search of the apartment yielded no clues or murder weapon—nor did he find Vanessa's backpack.

"Okay, time to get the police," he said out loud, backing slowly out of the apartment.

Just as he reached the door, he felt a gun jabbed into his back!

"Freeze!" a harsh voice shouted. "Don't move a muscle. You're under arrest!"

Chapter

3

JOE RAISED HIS HANDS over his head and felt someone cuff them together. "Up against the wall," a harsh voice commanded.

Peering back over his shoulder, he saw that it was an officer—a big, tall, muscular man of about fifty who sported a midriff bulge. A long scar ran down the right side of his forehead, and his eyes were dark and deep-set.

"Nothin' worth stealin' in here," he said, frisking Joe for weapons. "What did you think you were doin'?"

"I came to see Billy Barta," Joe explained. "But he's dead."

"Huh?"

"Over on the floor behind the couch," Joe said.

The officer went to look. He bent down over the body, then slowly straightened up. "Not a pretty sight. Okay, let's go down to head-quarters."

Joe swallowed hard. "Whatever you say, Officer. But I didn't kill anybody. I just came here to give Billy—"

"You can tell me your story on the way," the man interrupted. "But just remember—anything you say can be used against you."

Two hours later Joe had been fingerprinted and had his mug shots taken. He'd used his one phone call to contact Frank and the others at the party. Catlin had immediately headed for home in a cab to talk things over with her aunt Violet. Frank and Vanessa had driven down to NOPD Headquarters, where they now sat on a bench with Joe, who was being questioned by the tall, burly officer who'd made the arrest, Captain Brian Tomas.

"I understand what y'all are sayin'," Captain Tomas said patiently, pacing the bare, concrete interrogation room. "But there wasn't any other backpack in the apartment or in the deceased's car. I had my men check it out."

"But Joe's telling the truth!" Vanessa insisted.

The big detective swirled a cup of coffee around in his hand before swallowing its contents. "Billy Barta was under surveillance. In fact,

23

I was stakin' out his place myself tonight. Just so happened I went down to the corner to get a cup o' java, and when I came back, I saw the gate had been opened."

"Wait a minute, sir," Frank said. "You say Billy Barta was under surveillance. Why?"

The captain eyed Frank warily. "I can't say anythin' about that," he told him. "And maybe you already know. I hope for your sake you don't."

"I have no idea what you're talking about," Frank cried. "And neither does Vanessa or Joe."

"Maybe not," Tomas said with a shrug. "All I know is, I came back to the apartment and found Billy's body. Your brother was tryin' to sneak out of the place."

"Look, Officer Tomas," Vanessa broke in.

"Captain Tomas," he corrected her.

"Captain Tomas—Frank, Joe, and I are only down here for five days. We came for the Computer Horizons show and a little R and R. We met Billy at the show. We'd never laid eyes on him before!"

"It's the truth," Frank added.

"If it's the truth," Tomas began with a searching look in his eye, "then why's the other backpack missing?"

"I have no idea, sir," Joe said, fighting down the panic and anger that were rising in his throat. "All I know is, I couldn't reach Billy on the phone, and since our party was just a few blocks away, I walked over to see if I could get it back. I found him lying there, and I was just on my way to call the police when you found me."

"Uh-huh." Tomas didn't sound convinced. He checked his watch. "I'm going to talk this one over with my superiors." He walked out into the hallway.

"Can you believe this?" Frank said, shaking his head.

"And what about Billy," Vanessa added. "I wonder what he was up to for the police to be checking him out."

"Whatever it was, Captain Tomas isn't about to tell us," Frank commented.

At that moment Tomas came back into the room. "Chief of detectives is gone for the night," he told them. "The way I see it, even if your story's true, you're guilty of trespassin', maybe even breakin' and enterin'. I'm not going to charge you with murder, but I *am* going to keep you here overnight on suspicion."

"What?" Joe shouted, springing to his feet. "But I told you—"

"I know what you told me," Tomas said calmly. "And when the chief of detectives gets back in the mornin', I'll run things by him. Meanwhile, the lockup here's not too bad."

"Wait a second," Frank said. "What about us? You don't expect us to just go home, do you?"

"You can come back about nine in the mornin'," Tomas said. "I advise you to get yourselves a good night's sleep. There'll be time in the mornin' to get your brother a lawyer."

Seeing that there was no way around the patient but unmoveable Captain Tomas, Frank and Vanessa reluctantly said goodbye to Joe.

"Don't worry about me," Joe told them, trying to sound confident. "I'll be okay. I didn't do anything, and they can't charge me without evidence. I'll see you at nine."

Frank put his arms on Joe's shoulders. "Sure you're okay?" he asked in a low voice.

"Me?" Joe asked, patting Frank on the cheek. "Hey, I love lockups. A good, hard bed is great for the back."

Joe spent a restless night in the lockup. At eight A.M., Captain Tomas came into his cell, accompanied by a big man in a gray suit with thinning gray hair and a drooping mustache. "Is this the guy?" Tomas asked the man.

"That's him!" the man said angrily, pointing at Joe, who was just rubbing the sleep out of his eyes. "That's the guy who started the fight with Billy the other night at Tipitina's! I'd recognize that face anywhere!"

Tomas nodded gravely. "Okay, Mr. Stolarz," he said to the man. "You can wait up front. We'll draw up an affidavit for you to sign."

As the man in the gray suit left, he was still glaring angrily at Joe. "Stolarz?" Joe said, trying to place the name.

"Billy Barta's boss," Tomas said, sitting down next to Joe on the cot. "Look, do you want to make a confession now?"

"A confession?" Joe repeated, stunned.

"Look, you seem like a nice kid, and I hate to pin a murder rap on a guy with his whole life ahead of him. But I've got to look at the facts. Billy Barta made a play for your girlfriend. You got mad and tried to slug him. Looks to me like you got a good old-fashioned motive for murder. All's I need now's a weapon."

"You can't be serious!" Joe gasped.

"I wouldn't kid around about a thing like this," Tomas said. "See, I've been watchin' Billy, like I told you. At first, I figured he got killed over that other stuff. Jealousy never even occurred to me till I checked with Mr. Stolarz and he told me about the fight at Tipitina's."

"That's funny," Joe said, still trying to get his head clear. "I don't remember Stolarz being there."

"Well, there's always a crowd at that place," Tomas said. "You'd better call your brother and tell him to get you a lawyer. 'Cause I'm not lettin' you out of here."

"They're not going to let Joe go!" Frank said as he hung up the phone. He, Vanessa, Catlin, and Aunt Violet were standing anxiously in the kitchen.

"Do you think they can charge Joe?" Catlin asked.

"They can if they want to," Frank said. "Although they'll probably want to build a stronger case first. At any rate they're going to hold him as long as they can. Joe said they've set up a bail hearing for ten-thirty this morning. Unless we can raise the bond by then, he stays where he is."

"Maybe you should call your dad," Vanessa suggested.

"He's out of town on a case," Frank told her. "I could probably track him down if I had to, but first let's try to get Joe cleared ourselves."

"What about your mom?" Vanessa asked.

"I don't want to get her all upset," Frank said. "We're not due back till Wednesday, and it's only Monday morning. If we haven't cleared things up by then, there'll be plenty of time to call her. The important thing now is to get Joe out of jail so we can find out who really killed Billy Barta."

"How are we going to do that?" Vanessa asked.

"Maybe I can help," Aunt Violet said, reaching for a small but thick black book of phone numbers. "I'm pretty well connected in this town," she explained with a cryptic smile. She thumbed through the pages, which were crammed with entries. "And I think I know someone who might be able to help. . . ."

At ten-thirty Joe was led into a small, carpeted courtroom, where a stout, elderly judge waited, glancing over the files Captain Tomas had given her. "Ten thousand dollars bail sounds reasonable," the judge said. "Can you raise the bond, Mr. Hardy?"

Joe swallowed hard at the thought of spending the rest of his vacation in jail. He was about to say that he couldn't raise it when Frank and Vanessa burst into the room. They were followed by an extremely fat man in a wrinkled blue suit, who was wiping the sweat off his profusely perspiring forehead with a handkerchief. In his other hand, the man held an old, battered briefcase, which he slammed down on the table in front of the judge.

"Hello, Al," the judge said with a smile. "How's business? You come to bail out this boy?"

"That's right, Your Honor," the fat man said. Turning to Joe, he extended a chubby hand. "Name's Al," he said. "All-Night Al. I'm an old friend of Violet's. You got friends in high places, sonny."

All-Night Al snapped open his briefcase and looked up at the judge. "How much is bail, Your Honor?" he asked.

"Ten thousand," the judge replied.

"For breaking and entering?" Al asked. "Isn't that kinda steep?"

"There's also suspicion of murder here," Captain Tomas pointed out. "Just because we can't prove it yet doesn't mean we want the young man goin' free."

"I see." Al whistled softly, shaking his head. "Ah, well. What a man won't do for love," he said under his breath. "All right, Your Honor. Ten thousand it is."

A few minutes later Joe had been released with a ten thousand dollar bond posted by All-Night Al.

"Stick around," Captain Tomas warned Joe sternly as he walked them all to the front door. "Personally, I've got nothin' against you, y'understand. And Billy Barta wasn't exactly a Boy Scout. Still, murder's murder, so you'd better be here when I want you."

Joe nodded gravely and shook the officer's hand. Then he followed the others out the door into the warm New Orleans sunshine. They stood at the top of a wide stone staircase leading down to the street, which was packed with lawyers.

All-Night Al turned to Joe. "Looky here," he said, shaking his handkerchief at him. "That's ten thousand of my money got you out of there. You run, and my money goes with you. You get in trouble, and my money does, too. My money and I like it 'round here, and we don't like trouble. You all right with that?"

"Yes, sir," Joe said humbly. "Thanks for everything."

"Don't thank me," Al said, waving him off. "Thank Violet. She seems to have a soft spot for you, sonny—and I guess she knows somethin' about people after all these years of dealin' with them. Yes, she's quite a woman, Violet. Ain't seen me in seven years, and she can still talk me 'round her little finger!" Shaking his head in admiration, Al walked down the steps and along the avenue.

"Something tells me," Joe said, watching the fat man go, "that All-Night Al is one guy I wouldn't want to cross."

"Well," Frank said, "what do we do next?"

"I'll tell you what we do," Joe said, suddenly gripping Frank's arm and pointing to the crowded sidewalk. "See that guy down there, coming out of the coffee shop across the street? The one with the gray suit and mustache? That's Ron Stolarz, Billy Barta's boss. He's the one who fingered me for fighting with Billy!"

"That guy?" Frank asked, shading his eyes to get a better look. "I don't remember seeing him at Tipitina's."

"Me neither," Joe said, gritting his teeth.

Stolarz was walking quickly, headed for the corner of St. Charles Street, weaving his way through the crowd. "Let's go!" Frank said, and in an instant the trio was running down the stone steps after him. "Vanessa, you go get the car and head back to Violet's—tell them what happened. We'll take the streetcar back and meet you there."

The Hardys took off after Stolarz, but at the bottom of the steps, they ran smack into a river of pedestrians, most of whom were moving in the wrong direction. It was all they could do to keep Stolarz in sight. "Look, Frank!" Joe said. "He's getting on the St. Charles streetcar!"

The boys raced to the corner, where the old iron trolley was just pulling onto the Esplanade and gathering speed. Joe barely made it, leaping aboard at the last minute. Standing in the door of the streetcar, he turned around and reached out for Frank, who was out of breath. The streetcar was moving too fast and pulled away from him.

Joe turned and tried to spot Stolarz, but he couldn't see past the people packed tightly between him and the rest of the car. There was no way he could push his way through, either. He'd just have to keep an eye out for every stop, to see where Stolarz got off.

Just as he turned back around, Joe felt a hand

jam into his back. He grabbed for the guardrail but missed it, and flew off the streetcar.

For a second he felt nothing at all, but then he hit the pavement and a wave of pain shot through his head. He saw bright lights in front of his eyes and heard the sound of the streetcar fading away.

Then everything went black.

Chapter

4

FRANK STARTED TO RUN even before his brother hit the ground. By the time Joe landed he was close enough to hear the horrible sound of Joe's head hitting the street. The streetcar headed on up St. Charles.

"Joe!" Frank gasped, holding his brother's head in his hands. "Are you all right?"

Joe was unconscious, though. "Somebody call an ambulance!" Frank yelled. Joe's pulse was okay, and there was no blood, Frank noted with relief. But there *was* a nasty welt on his head.

Five minutes later the ambulance arrived. It was only on the ride to the hospital that Joe came to.

"Looks like a concussion," one of the paramedics told Frank. "But we'll know better after they look him over in emergency."

"Frank," Joe said in a soft whisper. "Stolarz—"

"It wasn't Stolarz who pushed you, Joe," Frank told him. "Just as you were shoved, I saw Stolarz leaning out one of the front windows of the trolley. Obviously, someone else didn't want us following Stolarz," Frank said. "But who?"

By the time Joe was released from the hospital, it was midafternoon. The doctors had given him a clean bill of health but told him to take it easy for a few days. Catlin and Vanessa drove down to take the boys back to the Garden District.

Aunt Violet ministered to Joe like an angel of mercy. She brought him tea and beignets, aspirin and extra pillows. Then she regaled him with stories about her days dating All-Night Al, back when he was still thin and a private detective. She even showed Joe an old photo of her and Al together. Violet had been an absolute knockout, Joe thought to himself. Al didn't look half bad himself.

"I nursed *him* back to health a couple of times, too," she told Joe.

By six o'clock he felt well enough to join his friends for one of Aunt Violet's huge, home-cooked dinners.

"Glad to see you're yourself again," Frank

said, as Joe took his seat. "I was pretty worried there for a while."

"Don't worry," Joe assured him with a nod toward Violet. "I'm in good hands."

"Think we can get busy again tomorrow morning?" Frank asked. "No time to waste if we're going to get you cleared."

"I'll be ready," Joe said.

Eight hours of sleep left Joe feeling good, and over breakfast the next morning the four young people sat around discussing what their next move should be.

"I think we ought to check out Stolarz first," Joe said, tearing into a stack of blueberry pancakes. "He must be up to something—why else would I get thrown off that streetcar?"

"Besides," Vanessa added, "none of us saw him at Tipitina's, yet he told the police he was there!"

Frank cautioned, "I don't think all of us going down to check out his warehouse in broad daylight is a good idea, though. Besides, there's another angle I'm even more curious about—why did the police have Billy Barta under surveillance?"

"You're not going to find out from Captain Tomas," Joe said, pouring himself a glass of orange juice. "He made it pretty clear that it was none of my business."

"We could ask around—question Billy's neighbors," Vanessa suggested.

"I don't know," Joe said warily. "Tomas warned me to stay out of trouble. And the police are probably swarming around Billy's place."

"I could go!" Catlin said excitedly. "They've never seen me. Maybe I could find out something!"

"You be safe, child!" Aunt Violet warned, poking her head in from the kitchen. "One person's been killed already." Then, dropping her stern demeanor, she smiled and added, "Besides, I've got a better idea for y'all."

"What's that, Aunt Violet?" Frank asked.

"Well," Violet said, wiping her hands on her apron, "they say that in Big Easy, everybody comes out for a good funeral."

"Of course!" Frank exclaimed, snapping his fingers. "Billy Barta's funeral! Why didn't we think of that?"

Joe had already grabbed that morning's paper and was leafing through the obituaries. "It says here that the medical examiner released Billy's body yesterday, and the funeral is today—two o'clock at Metairie Cemetery."

"I've got a few friends buried there myself," Aunt Violet said. "One of my old police beaus, from when I was a social worker for the force. At Metairie all the graves are up above ground,

37

'cause of the high water table 'round here. They can't dig two feet without hitting water."

"Sounds spooky," Vanessa said, making a face.

"Not as spooky as what you young people have been up to," Aunt Violet said pointedly. "Now y'all be careful, you hear? I don't want to have to go out there for any more funerals."

The cemetery was eerily beautiful. Everywhere Frank looked there were elaborate old vaults and tombs whose etched inscriptions had been worn away. Moss grew all around, even on the gravestones, and the willows truly seemed to weep.

Billy Barta clearly didn't have many friends. The mourners were a small, quiet group, many of them young, pretty women. Ron Stolarz was the only person Frank recognized. The priest intoned the service without emotion.

Looking around, Frank's attention was drawn to an elderly woman who hung back from the small crowd as the coffin was slipped into its vault. The woman's white hair blew wildly in the afternoon breeze, and she was staring at the coffin with a look of deep, dark hatred.

"Joe!" Frank whispered, elbowing his brother.

"I see her," Joe whispered back. Together, the brothers strolled toward the woman as the burial ended and the crowd began to disperse.

She was already walking away from them, and as they got closer Frank could hear her muttering to herself, "That *cochon*—he deserved to die for what he did."

Beside them, a pretty young brunette woman who must have also heard the old woman's words said to her companion, "That Denise LeMieux never gives up, does she? She swore she'd see Billy buried. I guess her predictions really do come true."

Turning back toward the old woman, Frank was astonished to find that she had vanished into thin air, or at least, into the late afternoon mists, which were creeping up from the bayous.

Glancing back at the gravesite in search of Ron Stolarz, Frank saw with disappointment that Ron, too, had disappeared. Another opportunity missed, Frank thought. He decided to seize the chance to find out about the weird old woman, so he approached the brown-haired woman and asked her about Denise LeMieux.

"She's got a little fortune-telling shop in the French Quarter," the young woman said, dabbing her eyes. "I think she's strange. I mean, to show up at poor Billy's funeral when everyone knows she's glad to see him dead."

Joe had joined them by now. "Glad? Why?" he asked.

"Well, Billy was there when her son died," the woman said. "I don't know what happened exactly, but she always blamed him for it." The young woman sighed. "Poor Billy! Why did this have to happen to him?"

Frank and Joe watched the two women go, then found Catlin and Vanessa, and told them what they'd heard. "Cool!" Vanessa said excitedly. "A mysterious suspect who can tell the future!"

"Uh, Vanessa," Joe said, arching an eyebrow, "Don't tell me you believe in that stuff."

"Of course I do," Vanessa proclaimed teasingly.

"I know!" Catlin jumped in. "Why don't we all go down to the old lady's place and get her to tell our fortunes?"

"Aw, come on," Joe groaned. "Get real."

"Maybe it's not such a bad idea, Joe," Frank said thoughtfully. "After all, Denise LeMieux is a legitimate suspect. According to what that girl said, the old lady hated Billy Barta."

"Yeah," Joe agreed. "But can't we investigate her some other way? I'd feel stupid getting my palm read."

"Oh, come on, spoilsport," Vanessa chided him.

"Joe?" Frank asked. "What do you say?"

Joe heaved a reluctant sigh. "Oh, okay. I guess I can try anything once—especially if it will clear me of murder."

It was five o'clock by the time Joe, Frank, and Vanessa returned to the French Quarter in search of Denise LeMieux's fortune-telling parlor. Catlin had had to go home to run errands for her aunt. Disappointed, Catlin had wished them luck and had taken the streetcar home.

A hot wind blew through Jackson Square, with its sidewalk cafés and artists. Walking down a narrow street off the square, Joe noticed a large sign featuring a devil's face with red smoke blowing out of its mouth. "Is that the place?" he asked. The sign said Voodoo Museum and Curio Shop.

"No, silly," Vanessa said. "Voodoo is voodoo—fortune-telling is totally different."

"It's all the same mumbo jumbo to me," Joe groused.

"Oh, come on," Vanessa said with a giggle. "Keep an open mind for once."

"Why?" Joe asked. "So she can see into it?"

"It should be on this block somewhere," Frank said, checking the slip of paper where he'd written the address. "Number 107½ . . ."

"Billy's apartment had a half in the number, too," Joe said. "And it was around the back. Maybe it's the same here."

Sure enough, they soon found a sign that said Madame LeMieux's Fortune-Telling Parlor: Your Future Seen Plain.

"Oh, brother," Joe said, shaking his head.

The three of them walked down a narrow brick alleyway to the back of the building, where they found a small black door with two hand painted green eyes staring out at them from above a large brass knocker. Joe couldn't help but feel that the eyes were staring right through him as he knocked.

They waited. "Maybe she's not home," Joe said hopefully.

But just then, the door swung slowly inward, creaking horribly. Madame LeMieux stared at Joe and the others with the same eerie green eyes that were painted on the door. "Come in," she said in a low, rattling voice. "Cross my palm with silver, and I will read your future for you."

Joe flashed Frank and Vanessa a quick grin to show what he thought of the old lady's tone of voice, then walked past her into the room.

The fortune-teller's den was dimly lit and smelled of incense. Pictures on the wall of figures from the tarot stared down at them—a death's head, a high priestess, and a man pierced by ten swords. "She ought to get herself a decorator," Joe whispered to Frank.

"So!" Denise LeMieux said to them as she shut the door. She faced them, a faint smile on her pale, wrinkled face. Joe noticed that a dark streak ran through her hair on one side, as if someone had painted it there. "What can I do for you? Tea leaves? Your palms read? Perhaps the cards would suit you. Yes, the tarot knows all. Tell me, which of you would like to be first?"

"He would," Vanessa said, shoving Joe forward.

Joe shot her a look, but said nothing. "Come, sit down, all of you," Madame LeMieux instructed. "Here, young man—shuffle this deck until you feel it has absorbed your energy. Then divide the deck into three piles."

Joe did as he was told, telling himself that the whole thing was a stupid waste of time, and that it was ridiculous to feel as weirded out as he did. When he had finished laying out the cards, the fortune-teller waved her hands over the piles, mumbling to herself in French, then turned over the top card of the first pile. A hideous devil glared up at Joe. He felt a chill run down his spine.

"What does it mean?" Joe asked.

"The Devil means mischief, suspicion, darkness, and double-dealing," the psychic said softly. "You have embarked upon a dangerous course. Beware of the Devil—it holds danger for you!"

"Uh-huh," Joe said slowly, stealing a dubious glance at Frank. "Why don't we go on to the next card?"

The old woman nodded, smiling her cryptic smile, and turned over the top card in the second pile. It showed a king, surrounded by five-pointed stars. Madame LeMieux's eyes lit up. "The King of Pentacles!" she said impressively. "How fortunate for you! Hidden riches lie beneath the surface. But you must face great hardships to earn them."

"And the third card?" Joe asked, totally engrossed now.

Madame LeMieux turned over the third card. It showed a tall castle tower with flames shooting out of its windows. "The Tower!" the old woman said darkly.

"What does it mean?" Joe asked, swallowing hard.

"The fire consumes all," she said, her green eyes widening and staring off into the distance as if she could see the future, one which only held horror. "Beware. Fire is your enemy."

Then Madame LeMieux gathered the remaining cards into a single pile and said, "Pick one. It will be your guide. Your future is troubled, and you will need it."

Joe closed his eyes and reached for a card. He turned it over. A four-pointed star!

"Ahh!" Madame LeMieux gasped. "The Star! You are very fortunate. You must be guided by the stars. When they shine down on you, you cannot fail. But beware when the mists come, for hidden within them lies mortal danger."

As Joe continued to stare at her, openmouthed, Madame LeMieux's expression changed. She smiled, held out her palm, and said, "That will be ten dollars, please. Which of you is next?"

Frank and Vanessa looked at each other while Joe fished in his pockets for a ten-dollar bill.

Madame LeMieux's eyes narrowed as she accepted the bill. She slowly opened a drawer and put the bill inside.

But when her hand came out again, there was a pearl-handled revolver in it—pointed straight at Joe's head!

Chapter

5

DENISE LEMIEUX'S EYES were wild with fury, but the gun in her hands was steady.

"You think I didn't recognize you from the funeral?" she asked. "When I blow your brains out, you won't think so much anymore. I know who you are, and I'm sick of you reporters pokin' your noses in my business!"

"Reporters?" Vanessa repeated.

"You need a little scare, all of you jackals who tear at people's wounds so they never heal." She came around from behind her table. "My son is dead!"

"We're not reporters, ma'am," Joe said. "We're here because the police think I killed Billy Barta!"

It was a gamble, and Joe knew it, but it paid off. The gun started shaking in the old woman's hand. With a sudden cry, she dropped it onto the table.

The old woman's sobs shook her sunken frame as if she were a rag doll. Joe helped her to a chair, while Vanessa poured her some water from a pitcher nearby.

"My boy, my Antoine..." Denise LeMieux rested her forehead on her palm. "He was my only child, a good boy until he hooked up with that Billy Barta!" She looked up at Joe, shaking her head knowingly. "You didn't kill him."

"No, ma'am," Joe said, trying to size up Denise LeMieux. She was old, all right, and frail. But her fury made her strong. Had it made her strong enough to kill Billy Barta?

"You want to find out who killed Billy, then," Madame LeMieux said, nodding. "Why should I help you? I'm glad he's dead. If not for him, my boy would still be alive."

"Could you tell us how your son died?" Frank asked.

Madame LeMieux sighed with grief and got to her feet. "I'll do better than that—I'll show you." Beckoning for them to follow, she led them past a beaded curtain, into the rear of the shabby apartment.

"This is Antoine's room," she said, ushering them into a tiny bedroom. "It's just like he left it—except for all the pictures. Sometimes he talks to me when I'm in here."

Joe and Frank exchanged wary glances.

"How did your son know Billy?" Frank asked.

"They met in the Quarter, during Mardi Gras," the old woman said, passing a picture of Antoine to them.

Joe took it and studied it. A sandy-haired young man with a drooping mustache stared back at him.

"He used to go out on Lake Pontchartrain, fishing at night," Denise LeMieux said. "But what he did out there with Billy wasn't fishing. Billy would come over here with a lot of money and try to get Antoine to go into business with him. Antoine always said no, he told me. But I don't know. Maybe that's why he ended up dead." She wiped away a stray tear before continuing.

"One night about eight months back, Antoine didn't come home. And in the morning the police come 'round to tell me he was run over by a boat while he was in the water." She sobbed and sank onto the bed. Vanessa sat down next to her, and put a comforting arm around the old woman's shoulders.

"Those police is no better than the crooks!" the fortune-teller continued bitterly. "Every time I tried to tell them it weren't no accident, that Billy Barta had gotten my boy into something evil, they'd say 'Yes, ma'am, we'll look into it.' But nothin' ever come of it."

Joe looked over at Frank. He knew they were both thinking the same thing. If *they* had been the police and a woman like Denise LeMieux had come to them with her suspicions, they probably wouldn't have taken her too seriously, either.

"And Billy Barta was with your son the night he died?" Frank asked.

"He was there all right," Madame LeMieux replied. "They went out on Billy's boat that night. Billy's the one who told the police what happened. I know he was in on my son's murder. And I'm glad Billy Barta's dead."

"Is there anything else you can tell us that might help us clear my brother?" Frank asked.

Madame LeMieux raised her head and gave them all the strangest look. "What I know is for me to know. The cards tell me the truth. Only *people* lie."

Joe cleared his throat. "Well, I guess we'd better go. We've bothered you long enough."

Just as they reached the front door, Madame LeMieux appeared at the beaded curtain. "Those were your cards, and that is your fortune, my boy," she said, staring at Joe intently. "Beware of the Devil, look for treasure beneath the surface, watch out for fire and the mist—and remember, the stars are your friends!"

Outside, the three of them took deep breaths

of fresh air. "Whew!" Vanessa said. "She was really strange. Do you think she could have killed Billy?"

"I don't know," Frank said.

"Now what?" Joe asked, as they reached the street.

"It all seems to lead in one direction," Frank said. "Billy Barta. What kind of 'business' was he doing out on the lake? What kind of 'business calls' was he going home to make the day he was murdered? And why did the police have him under surveillance? What did they suspect?"

"Too bad Tomas won't tell us," Joe said.

"Let's go see him right now," Frank suggested. "Maybe I can persuade him to talk."

It was a short drive to NOPD Headquarters, and luckily, Captain Tomas was in. He was in the bullpen, where the officers waited to receive their assignments.

Frank started by telling the captain all about Denise LeMieux, but Tomas remained unconvinced. "Listen," he said, "if you're tryin' to hand me Denise LeMieux as a suspect in Billy Barta's murder, you're not tellin' me anything new. She's got motive, and maybe opportunity, too. But somehow, I don't see her knockin' Billy's block off. As far as I'm concerned, your brother's still my number one suspect. And I don't tell my suspects anything they don't need to know—like why Billy Barta was under surveillance."

"But what about Antoine LeMieux's death?" Frank asked. "Are you so sure it was an accident?"

Captain Tomas was clearly losing patience. "Look," he said, grabbing his hat as he prepared to leave, "I was in charge of the LeMieux investigation, and it was definitely an accident. Unlike Billy's death."

Turning to Joe, he added, "I don't know if you're guilty, but I am puttin' a case together. And if you killed Billy, you're goin' to pay. Now, today's Monday. I'll fish around for other suspects till Thursday. If I don't find any by then, I'm takin' you in. That clear?" Jamming his hat on his head, Captain Tomas strode out the door, leaving them to stare after him.

"Great work," Joe said wryly. "Aren't you thrilled we came down here again?"

"Let's head back," Frank responded, ignoring the dig. "I'm getting hungry, and it's already seven."

They left the building, got into their rental car, and pulled into traffic. All three were silent until they'd gone about half a mile, when Frank peered into the rearview mirror and said, "Don't look now, but we're being followed."

"The police?" Vanessa asked, turning around.

"Just a plain black sedan," Frank said.

"Whoever it is, we can't lead them back to Violet's," Joe pointed out. "Turn around, Frank, and let's lose them."

"Good idea," Frank said, executing a fast right turn onto a narrow side street. The black sedan stayed with them.

Frank made several more quick turns, but the black sedan only got closer. Finally seeing a ramp with a sign that said HWY. 39, ST. BERNARD, he took it. "Maybe we can get up a little speed on the highway and lose them," he said.

Unfortunately, Highway 39 to St. Bernard turned out to be a two-lane road leading straight into bayou country, with no turnoffs whatsoever. On either side of the road were deep ditches. Beyond the ditches were narrow levees, and beyond them, the shallow, murky water of the bayous.

The sun had gone down now, and the evening mists were thicker out in the country than they were in town. It got harder and harder to see the road, but Frank could still make out those two headlights in his mirror.

"Faster, Frank!" Joe said. "They're still behind us!"

"If I go any faster," Frank retorted, "I'm likely to go off the road. I can't see a thing out here!"

It was almost totally dark now. Joe thought back to what Madame LeMieux had warned—to beware of the mist. Was she a true psychic? he wondered. Or had she known something she wasn't telling them?

"Look out, Frank!" Vanessa suddenly shouted

as a deer materialized on the road in front of them. Frank swerved to the right, avoiding the terrified animal just in time. But when Frank yanked the wheel left again, it was too late. The car skidded right off the narrow road.

"Hold on!" Frank shouted. "We're going to hit the water!"

Chapter
6

THE CAR PLUNGED off the road and into the mud, moss, and black water of the ditch. It hit with a tremendous splash. Then, for long, agonizing seconds, there was dead silence.

"Everybody all right?" Frank finally asked.

"I think so," Vanessa said.

"Nice driving, Frank," Joe said. "Next time, let me take over."

"Let's just hope there aren't any alligators here," Frank replied.

But then the screech of tires reminded them that there were more immediate dangers. Their pursuers had arrived.

"I'll get the tire iron out of the trunk," Frank said.

The three of them emerged from the car, which was stuck in mud a foot deep, and shielded their eyes from the glare of the headlights shining down on them from the road above.

In those headlights, the silhouette of a huge, menacing figure loomed over them. Sloshing through the muck, Frank made his way to the trunk and quickly retrieved the tire iron. "What do you want?" Frank shouted, brandishing his weapon.

"You didn't really want to leave me and N'Orleans behind, now did you, Mr. Hardy?" a familiar voice boomed.

"All-Night Al!" Joe gasped. "Am I glad it's you! At least, I *think* I'm glad."

"If you were trying to hoof it out of town, you're definitely not going to be glad," Al's voice rang out.

"We saw you following us," Frank explained. "But we didn't know who it was—and we didn't want to lead whoever it was to Violet's house."

"That's some good thinkin'," Al said, his tone softening. "But who did you think might be followin' you? The cops?"

"Somebody's already tried to kill Joe once," Frank said. "He got shoved off a streetcar."

"Well, that can happen," Al said. "Anyhow, lemme help y'all outta that swamp. You're gonna need a car wash."

"Why were you following us in the first place?"

Vanessa asked as Al picked his way down the bank.

"Been trailin' you all day," Al said. "Wanted to make sure Handsome Joe here didn't decide to vanish. When y'all headed out onto Highway Thirty-Nine, I thought I'd better run you down."

"Do you pull this kind of stunt with all the people you bail out?" Joe asked sardonically.

Al shot him an annoyed glance. "I told you, Violet's an old friend o' mine. And like I said, she's got a soft spot for you. I wouldn't want to see you let the lady down."

Soon, with the pull of a strong chain Al had in his trunk, the Hardys' car was back on the road, and they were on their way to Violet's house, with Al tailing them still.

"Oh, my goodness, just look at y'all!" Violet said when she saw their muddy pants and shoes. "You been diggin' for crawdads or somethin'?" Then she cracked a smile. "I bet you're hungry. I can grill you some burgers. Al, did you have your dinner?"

"I'd be obliged to stay, Violet," Al said, a broad grin settling over his pudgy face. "I do love a good burger."

After dinner everybody sat for a while in the dining room. "You boys and Vanessa had better call your parents and tell them what's going on," she said.

"You heard the lady," Al said. "Get on the phone."

Speaking to their mom, Joe and Frank tried to soft-pedal what had happened over the past two days. But when Laura Hardy heard why her sons weren't coming home on Wednesday, she got very upset. "I'm getting on the next plane to New Orleans."

"Now, Mom," Joe said, trying to calm her down, "you don't need to do that. It's a simple misunderstanding. We just need some time to clear it up."

"Joe's right, Mom," Frank said, speaking on the upstairs extension. "We would have called you before this if there was any need for you to get involved."

"I just wish your father was here," Laura Hardy said. "I get so worried about you boys sometimes."

"There's no need to worry, Mom," Frank assured her. "But we'll call you if it turns out we need Dad's help."

"He'll be back on Friday," their mom said. "Until then, don't take any foolish chances. Promise me."

"We promise," Joe said. After they hung up, the brothers went out to the veranda and sat in a pair of wicker chairs.

Soon, Al came outside to say good night. He had a blissful smile on his face. "It sure is good to see Violet again," he said. "Guess I have you fellas to thank for that."

"I gather you two were an item once," Frank said.

"A long time ago," Al told him. "Too late now to be revivin' any of that."

"Why?" Joe asked. "You're not married, are you?"

"Me?" Al asked, with a laugh. "No, I'm married to my job, and Violet's married to all her good causes. Besides, I'm too fat to interest a good-lookin' woman like her. Of course, maybe if I went on a diet . . ." He walked down the steps, contemplating the possibilities.

A few minutes later Vanessa came out to tell them she was going to sleep. Catlin and Violet were already in bed.

"Tired?" Frank asked Joe, checking his watch when Violet had gone.

"I'm totally exhausted," Joe replied, "but I couldn't sleep if I tried. I keep thinking about this case."

"So do I. And it keeps boiling down to Barta."

"Exactly," Joe said. "I didn't notice anything suspicious in his apartment that night, but I might have missed something. Do you think we could get in there?"

"We could cruise by," Frank suggested. "But the police probably have it cordoned off."

"How about Stolarz's warehouse?" Joe asked.

"You mean now?" Frank asked, raising his eyebrows.

"Probably pretty quiet down there, this time of night," Joe said casually.

"It's worth a shot," Frank said, getting to his feet. "Let's look up the address and go."

Ten minutes later, with Joe at the wheel this time, they pulled their muddy rental car off to the side of the road a block from the warehouse. It was one of a dozen or so buildings along the levee in the industrial section of the riverfront just outside the French Quarter. At the front of the warehouse stood a small booth with a security guard inside.

"How do we get in?" Joe asked Frank as they got out of the car and approached the building.

Frank surveyed the place—bars on all the windows, parking lot to the side, the river in back. "Let's go up the fire escape to the roof," he suggested, pointing to a set of iron stairs leading up from the parking lot side.

Giving the guard booth a wide berth, they entered the lot and crept close to the wall. There, Joe got on Frank's shoulders and pulled down the iron ladder as quietly as he could. Then they mounted the ladder and climbed to the roof.

"Awesome!" Joe exclaimed, turning to look at the incredible view. The building was only two stories high, but New Orleans was flat as a pancake and the boys could see the multicolored lights of the city spreading out for miles in every direction.

"That mist cleared off beautifully," Frank remarked.

"That means good luck," Joe told his brother.

"I thought you didn't believe in all that fortune-telling stuff," Frank said.

"After what happened in the fog tonight, I don't know," Joe told him. "Hey, look—let's try that skylight." Joe yanked at it, but the skylight was shut tight.

"Here," Frank said. "Try this tire iron. I brought it from the car, just in case."

Applying a little leverage, Joe soon had the skylight pried open. "Come on," he said, lowering himself through.

Grabbing a handhold on a girder, he dangled above the dark warehouse floor. He searched for a place to land. Seeing a pile of wooden packing crates, Joe swung himself back and forth until he could make it to the top of them. They swayed, but luckily didn't go over. From there, it was just a short climb down to the warehouse floor.

"Boy, is it dark in here!" Frank whispered as he jumped down beside Joe. "Joe, shine your flashlight around. Let's see if we can find where Billy's office is."

Joe pulled out his penlight and turned it on. "Yaaah!" he cried out loudly. The huge red-and-black face of the Devil was staring right at him!

"Shhhh!" Frank warned. "Take it easy, Joe! It's just one of the Mardi Gras floats they make here."

"Oh, yeah," Joe said softly, blowing out a breath of air. "I thought—oh, never mind what I thought."

" 'Beware of the Devil,' the old lady said."

"Don't remind me," Joe told him. "Aw, come on, it's just a coincidence. Let's go find Billy's office."

It was totally dark except for the beam from Joe's flashlight. If there was a security guard, he was nowhere in sight. Frank and Joe meandered around the huge warehouse floor, past floats of all kinds. There was one of Jean Lafitte, the famous pirate, and one of Elvis Presley. Finally they found a wall with several offices built into it. On one of the doors was a plastic plaque that said B. BARTA.

"This must be the place," Joe commented as Frank got out his trusty lock pick and jimmied the door open.

Billy's office was a mess, with papers strewn everywhere, drawers pulled open and their contents dumped on the floor. "Somebody's been here before us," Frank remarked. "Probably Stolarz."

"Hey, Frank, look at this," Joe said. He was standing over Billy's desk, where he'd shoved aside the pile of papers. On the blotter, Billy had obviously been doing some doodling. Joe read it out loud: " 'The King is dead. Long live the King.' "

Frank examined the scrawled writing. "Looks like he was just fooling around."

"But for some reason, I keep thinking of what Madame LeMieux said."

"Forget it," Frank told him. "Let's just concentrate on what's in front of us, huh? People doodle about what's on their minds. Besides, don't the words ring a bell?"

" 'The King . . .' " Joe repeated.

For a minute Frank remained lost in thought. Then suddenly he laughed out loud. "And he spelled *king* with a capital *K*. Hey, Joe—I've got it! There's an Elvis float out there on the floor. Elvis is 'The King,' right? It's worth a look."

In no time both boys were heading back across the warehouse floor. Then, abruptly, Frank stood still. "Cut your flashlight, Joe," he whispered. "I hear something."

Joe did as he was told and listened. Distant footsteps—probably a security guard, he guessed. He'd figured there had to be one.

The footsteps grew louder. Joe held his breath. Then they stopped. A flashlight played around the warehouse floor. It missed Joe and Frank by inches! Then the footsteps started up again and grew fainter and fainter. Frank tapped Joe on the shoulder, and the brothers crept forward again, still with no light. Just as they approached the Elvis float, Joe backed up to see if he could spot anyone coming.

In that moment he hit a toolbox and sent it crashing to the floor. Joe felt the blood begin to pound in his head. The crash had been deafening in the silent warehouse. Had anyone heard?

A metal door banged open against a far wall. "Who's there?" a voice sounded. A flashlight beam played across the floor and soon picked out the brothers. "Hey, George! We've got a break-in! Hold it right there, you two!" Two security guards came running toward them.

"Quick, Joe! Back the way we came!" Frank yelled.

The boys climbed back up the crates and caught hold of the girder as quickly as they could. Joe hauled himself through the skylight and onto the roof, and was just catching his breath when he heard a cry from Frank. "Joe, help me!"

Joe peered back through the skylight to find Frank dangling by one arm from the girder.

"I lost my grip!" Frank shouted. Below him, the two guards were drawing pistols from their holsters. Joe grabbed Frank by his free arm and dragged him through the skylight just as shots rang out from below.

"I guess we made it!" Frank said, standing up.

"Guess again, kid," came a harsh voice from behind him. "Back up, both of you—and put your hands over your heads!"

Chapter

7

WHEELING AROUND, FRANK SAW that a third security guard had gotten up to the roof ahead of them. He had his gun drawn and was backing them up against the retaining wall. Frank peeked back over his shoulder and over the wall.

Below them lay the river, two stories down. It would be a long jump, Frank knew. If the river was deep enough here to allow ships to dock, it had to be deep enough to dive into safely—he hoped. Anyway, it was either that or jail. He nodded subtly toward the wall.

"Freeze, I said!" the guard shouted.

"One, two, three . . ." Frank whispered. Like a precision machine, the brothers spun around in unison and jumped.

Frank felt the water hit him like a sledgehammer, knocking the air out of him. He came up spitting dirty river water and flailing blindly. "Joe!" he called out. "Are you all right?"

For a moment there was no response. Then Joe surfaced right next to Frank. "Whooee!" he yelled. "We made it!"

"The car's that way, I think."

When they emerged from the river onto the levee about two hundred yards downriver, they were coated with grime and oil from the water, and both of them stank.

"Doesn't look like anybody's following us," Frank said, shaking himself off. "That rental car is never going to be the same once we get into it though."

"Let's get back to Violet's and shower, quick," Joe said.

They drove with all the windows open. "That third guard was a nasty surprise," Frank said as they pulled up at Violet's.

"I know," Joe said, getting out of the car. "Hey, look—stars! Remember what Madame LeMieux said? Clear skies are my friend. The woman is uncanny."

"Come on now," Frank grumbled. "The skies are clear half the time. You can't make something out of that, Joe."

"But what about the fact that it was foggy earlier tonight when we ran off the road? And what about that Devil float in the warehouse?"

"Somehow I don't think that was exactly what she meant by 'Beware of the Devil.' " Frank said with a wry grin as they walked toward the front door.

"Maybe not," Joe said. "But I still think we ought to check out that Elvis float. Remember, Madame LeMieux said hidden riches lie beneath the surface. And the card she said it about was a king."

"Okay, okay, we'll try to get a closer look at it." Frank shook his head and laughed. "And this from the guy who thought fortune-telling was a lot of mumbo jumbo! Come on, Swami. Let's get cleaned up."

"I'll never forgive you two for this!" Vanessa said the next morning as they all sat wolfing down Aunt Violet's delicious breakfast crepes. "How could you go off and do something so incredibly dangerous without me?"

Joe shrugged. "It was just a spur of the moment thing."

"Don't give me that," Vanessa said, crossing her arms.

"Well, we're going back to the warehouse this morning," Joe said. "So if you want to come, now's your chance."

"This morning?" Vanessa repeated. "But, Joe,

Stolarz has already seen you—he'll never let you in the place."

"Joe's going to wait in the car," Frank explained. "I'm going in alone this time."

"No way!" Joe argued. "We go together, or not at all."

"Wait." Vanessa held up a hand. "I've got a better idea. Joe, why don't you try questioning Stolarz right up front? It only makes sense that you'd want to talk to him. And while you distract him, Frank and I can try to get at the Elvis float."

"Good idea!" Frank said, nodding.

"Hey, what about me?" Catlin interrupted.

"Cat," Vanessa said, "we need someone back here to stand by the phone in case there's any trouble."

"Aunt Vi can do that," Catlin said stubbornly.

"Uh-uh, no way," Aunt Violet called out from the kitchen. "I'm not going to sit around and worry till the rest of my hair turns gray. I'm going to look up an old friend and see if he can do somethin' for Joe."

Catlin sighed resignedly. "Oh, all right."

"Thanks, Cat," Vanessa said before turning to the Hardys. "Now, come on, you guys, let's get moving."

"Hey!" Joe complained. "I'm still eating!"

"Never mind," Vanessa insisted. "Too many

crepes will weigh you down. And we don't want that to happen, do we?"

After stopping at a grocery store off Jackson Square for some supplies, the Hardys and Vanessa pulled over to the side of the road within sight of the warehouse. Frank checked out his coconspirators as they emerged into the morning sunshine. "We're out of our minds for trying this," he said.

"Hey," Vanessa replied, "as the one who thought up this plan, I resent that remark."

"Besides, have you got a better idea?" Joe asked grimly.

Frank didn't answer. It was true—their options were limited, and so was their time. They had to take big chances.

Joe headed for the front door while Frank and Vanessa donned the white plastic hard hats and clipboards they'd bought on the way there that morning. The helmets bore the initials *EPA*, spray-painted in green.

"Is the paint dry yet?" Frank asked.

"I don't know. Just don't touch it," Vanessa advised.

"Let's hope they don't ask to see our credentials."

The warehouse was somehow less menacing during the day, Frank thought as he and Vanessa crossed the parking lot. They were headed for the loading doors at the back of the warehouse that led directly onto the riverbank. When the workers on the dock saw Frank and Vanessa, one of them went to get the boss, a huge man with thick muscles and a dull expression.

"G'morning," he said flatly. "What can I do for you?"

"EPA," Frank said, flashing his card case quickly and hoping the man wouldn't take a closer look at his ID. "We've received reports you may be using some carcinogenic solvents in the manufacturing of your Mardi Gras floats."

"We won't get in your way," Vanessa assured the man. "But we do have to take a look around."

"Who told you that?" the foreman asked, frowning. "I'll have to check with Mr. Stolarz."

"Oh, that's not necessary," Frank explained quickly. "We don't put too much credence in these rumors—but we do have to check them out. Just a formality, you understand."

"We don't have much time," Vanessa said, jumping in. "We've got a lot of places to check out this morning. We'll just be a few minutes, okay? You can go on about your business. We'll let you know if we spot any hazards."

The foreman thought it over. "Okay," he finally said. "Go wherever you want. We ain't got nothin' to hide. But make it quick. And I'm still going to tell the boss you're here." He led them inside, and then he headed up a flight of stairs to a catwalk leading to the front of the building, where Stolarz's office was located on the second floor.

"Great," Frank muttered under his breath. They wasted no time in going over to the area where the floats were stored and repaired. They nosed around in various paint cans and solvent bottles for as long as the foreman was in sight. As soon as he disappeared, they went straight to the Elvis float.

"You keep an eye on the workers," Frank said, "while I give the King a thorough examination."

At the front of the warehouse, Joe rang the bell on the side of the glass door and was buzzed in. He walked calmly into the gray-carpeted front office, stepped up to the receptionist, and asked to see Mr. Stolarz.

"May I tell him who's here to see him?" the receptionist asked, her penciled eyebrows arching.

"Joe Hardy," she said.

"And who are you with?" the receptionist asked.

"I was a friend of Billy Barta's."

That got the receptionist's attention. She buzzed Stolarz, and when he picked up the intercom, she said, "There's a Joe Hardy to see you, sir."

Listening to Stolarz's reply, the receptionist's

eyes widened. "Oh! I see!" she said. "Yes, sir. Of course!" Hanging up, she turned to Joe, her expression set. "I'm afraid—"

Joe was already past her, on his way up the stairs that led to the inner offices. "I'll just be a minute," he shouted over his shoulder. Before she could react, he had already reached the second floor and the door marked Ronald J. Stolarz, President.

"Hello, there!" Joe said, throwing open the door. The stunned and clearly furious warehouse owner rose from his desk. "We haven't been properly introduced—I'm Joe Hardy."

"I know who you are," Stolarz said, rearing up to his full height. "Who told you you could come in here?"

"Well, you see, the police think I killed Billy Barta, only it's not true, and I need to find out who really did—"

"You killed him, all right!" Stolarz fumed. "Now get out before I call the cops!"

"I was just curious," Joe breezed on fearlessly, "how you could have recognized me as the guy who fought with Billy at Tipitina's? You weren't even there."

Joe was bluffing, of course. He couldn't be sure Stolarz wasn't at Tipitina's. But the ploy worked. Stolarz stopped in his tracks, caught off guard by the accusation.

"I didn't think I saw you there," Joe said with a smile. "Thanks for confirming my suspicions."

"Why, I ought to—" Stolarz began advancing toward Joe.

"Now, now, Mr. Stolarz," Joe cautioned him. "I was hoping you could help me clear myself. And since you were so nice as to let me in here, just one more question—do you happen to know what Billy Barta was up to? I mean, you were aware the police had him under surveillance, weren't you? I'm sure he was trying to hide his activities from you, but since you're such an astute man, I just wondered—"

"GET OUT!" Stolarz bellowed, his face white with fury. Joe backed off, feeling he'd done all he could to give Frank and Vanessa the time they needed. It was time to retreat.

Joe found his way blocked by the huge bulk of Stolarz's foreman. "Some people here from the EPA, boss. Looking over our paints and solvents. I told them to go ahead, but I thought I'd better check with you."

"EPA?" Stolarz asked, confused. "They usually call to make an appointment. Go check their credentials, Ralph."

"Right, boss," the man said, giving Joe the once-over before leaving the room.

"Well, I'll be going," Joe said, turning and heading for the door before Stolarz had a chance to stop him.

Joe ran out into the sunshine and headed for the car, turning to make sure he wasn't being followed. He was worried about Frank and Vanessa. Something told him they were going to have to make a quick getaway—and he wanted to be ready when they ran for it.

Frank had already been all over the Elvis float and found nothing. He'd checked out the motor, the backing of the fiberglass body, the controls that made the figure wave its hand and swivel its gigantic hips.

Discouraged, Frank turned to Vanessa. "I don't know," he said. "Maybe this is a wild-goose chase. That foreman's going to be back any minute." He glanced up at the empty catwalk above them.

"Let me have a look," Vanessa said, climbing into the truck's cab.

"Go right ahead," Frank said, sitting down on Elvis's huge left foot. Frank shifted his weight and the foot shifted, too. Getting up, he examined it more closely and saw that the fiberglass shoe was hinged, and was actually the door to a hidden compartment. "Look, Van!" he said, holding up the foot with one hand. "There's a metal strongbox in here!"

Vanessa scrambled down from the cab and hovered close to Frank.

Fishing out his trusty lock pick and checking

to see that no one was looking, Frank jimmied open the strongbox, which was about twice the size of a fishing tackle case. It was bolted to the truck chassis on which the twenty-foot high statue of Elvis stood.

Frank threw open the top of the box and gasped. Inside, he saw a rack of computer circuit boards and a box of what looked like credit cards, except their surfaces were blank and shiny, and they had two tiny metal connectors at one end. Grabbing a card and one of the circuit boards, Frank closed the box and lowered Elvis's foot back into its original position.

"What are those?" Vanessa asked.

"Circuit boards—and some kind of card," Frank said.

"Didn't we see some of those cards at the show?"

"That's right," Frank acknowledged. "Real cutting edge technology."

"Why would you need cutting edge technology for a Mardi Gras float?" Vanessa wondered.

"You wouldn't!" Frank said, pocketing the board and the card. "That box is being hidden here, don't you see? And we're going to find out why."

"Hey, you two!" The foreman's angry voice froze them. "What do you think you're doing?"

Frank looked up to see the foreman on the

catwalk above them. "Stop those two!" he shouted.

Luckily, most of the workers were all the way across the warehouse. As the two of them tore across the floor, Frank looked back over his shoulder. To his horror, he realized that the huge Devil's head float was speeding after them. Any minute now they'd be crushed flat against the brick wall just ahead of them.

Chapter

8

THERE WAS NO TIME for Frank to shout out a warning, so he did the only thing possible—he shoved Vanessa sideways. She went sprawling into a pile of soft packing filler.

Frank was still in harm's way and the Devil float was bearing down on him fast. With a quick feint to his right, Frank suddenly veered left and leapt for some bales of hay that were used in building floats.

The feint worked. The driver of the truck made a hard right. When he saw that Frank had gone left, he spun his wheel in that direction. But the big, unwieldy vehicle was not made for that kind of maneuvering.

Flat on his back in the hay and completely

helpless, Frank watched as the Devil truck went over onto its right-hand wheels, and with a sickening skid, careened straight into one of the other floats—a huge bowl of tropical fruit surrounded by the smiling faces of Caribbean islanders. The happy faces went flying in all directions. A plastic eyeball the size of a basketball flew right at Frank, just missing him. Across the aisle, the Devil truck lay on its side, its wheels spinning as the driver crawled slowly out of the crushed cab.

"Vanessa! Quick—the emergency exit!" Frank yelled. He leapt to his feet, climbed over the disabled Elvis float, and broke into a run. Out of the corner of his eye, he could see that Vanessa was right behind him. Behind her, several workers were clambering over the float, shouting for the pair to stop.

Frank kicked open the emergency door and found himself at the threshold of the parking lot. Then, as soon as Vanessa was safely outside, he slammed the door behind them and dragged a heavy crate in front of it to slow down their pursuers. "Come on!" he shouted, leading Vanessa around the cars in the lot.

He spotted the rental car parked in the alley beyond the lot, and took off with Vanessa at his side. Just as they reached it and jumped inside, a security guard appeared at their tail end. Joe hit the accelerator, and the man was left banging on the rear of the car in a futile rage.

"Whew!" Joe said, when they'd left their pursuers behind. "Looks like you two made some people mad."

"We found something really interesting," Frank said. "A strongbox hidden inside Elvis's foot. And it was filled with circuit boards and other stuff."

"Like what?" Joe asked.

"Well, I'm not exactly sure," Frank said. "But I took one for a souvenir."

"Well, let's go someplace where we can grab a bite to eat and look at it," Joe replied.

They pulled into a seafood shack for oyster po' boys, and while they ate, Joe examined the circuit board and small card.

"The card is obviously something you run in a computer," Frank commented.

"What do you think is on it?" Vanessa asked.

"Something worth hiding, that's for sure," Frank told her. "In fact, it's probably been encoded for secrecy."

"Well, how can we find out what it is?" she asked.

Frank thought for a moment. "Hey, remember that company that had a table at the computer show where they were decoding cards like this?"

"Yeah," Joe said. "What was their name?"

"Decoders, Inc. They were based here in town,

too," Frank recalled. "Let's take this over to their offices right after lunch."

"I think our luck has finally turned," Joe said.

Frank frowned and said, "Let's hope you're right."

After lunch they checked the yellow pages and found the address for Decoders, Inc., then drove to Greenbriar Woods, a suburb. They found the small company at an unimposing storefront on a quiet side street.

"Come on, let's go inside," Frank said.

The gray-carpeted room was divided into prefabricated white cubicles, with only the tap-tapping of fingers on keyboards punctuating the silence. A skinny, sandy-haired young man wearing thick black-framed glasses got up from behind a desk and approached them. "My name's Jeffrey DeVine. How can I help you?"

Frank did the talking. "We've got a circuit board here, and a—"

"Flash memory card," DeVine finished for him as he glanced at what Frank was holding. "Would you like to have it decoded?"

"Sure thing," Frank said.

They followed him into a small office containing a large computer bank and a high-resolution color monitor. "Let's see what you've got here," he said, inserting the board and the card into the open back of the machine.

He keyed in a few commands, and they found

themselves looking at a screen full of diagrams. DeVine scrolled downward. There were more diagrams, along with charts, command sequences, and unintelligible programming language. "Now let's do some decoding," he said.

After a few minutes wait the decoding program DeVine used started doing its work. "Wow!" DeVine said slowly, squinting at the screen through his thick glasses and curling a lock of his hair around a finger. "You all in the defense industry?"

"Defense industry?" Joe asked. "What makes you think so?"

" 'Cause what you brought me appears to be a small part of an extremely advanced missile targeting system."

"You're kidding!" Vanessa gasped.

"No, ma'am, I wouldn't kid you," DeVine said excitedly. "You could put this in a cruise missile, give it an address anywhere in the world, and it would blow up the building."

Frank, Joe, and Vanessa stared at one another in disbelief. "No wonder they were all trying so hard to keep us away from there," Joe half-whispered.

"Er, thanks, Mr. DeVine," Frank said, taking back the card and the board. "What do we owe you?"

"Oh, nothing," DeVine said, smiling. "My

pleasure. It only took a few minutes, and anyway, it's not every day you see one of those."

"Thanks, Mr. DeVine," Frank said, stuffing the board and card into his backpack and heading outside. "We've got to turn this in to the police right away!"

"What's all this stuff?" Captain Tomas asked when Frank put the circuit board and the flash memory card on his desk. "You know, I'm tired of all these distractions from you kids. I'm not particularly eager to hear any of your wild stories. It's only Wednesday, but if you're here to confess, that's all right. Otherwise, make it quick and go back home till I come for you with a warrant. I should have it by tomorrow."

"But wait till you hear this," Joe said excitedly. "This board and flash memory card were hidden in Mr. Stolarz's warehouse! We had them decoded, and guess what?"

"I can't imagine," Tomas said laconically.

"They're part of a missile targeting system!" Joe finished. "Advanced weapons technology— they could even be government property, the kind of stuff that shouldn't go out of the country. Now you tell us, Captain Tomas, what would something like that be doing in Ron Stolarz's warehouse?"

Tomas acted momentarily taken aback. Then he sucked in a deep breath and blew it out, stood up and placed both hands on the desk. "I've got a better one for you," he said. "What were *you* doing in Mr. Stolarz's warehouse? Did you have an engraved invitation to look around there?"

Frank shot Joe a look that said he shouldn't have told the captain so much.

"Uh, well," Joe hedged, "I guess we did take a few liberties, sir. But if you'll just examine these, you'll see that it's a good thing we went in there. And there are a lot more of these in the warehouse. What if Stolarz plans to smuggle them out of the country or something?"

"Whoa, now," Tomas said, holding up a hand to stop him. "You're goin' way too fast for me. First of all, where am I supposed to look for the rest of the stuff?"

Frank stepped in. "In a strongbox under the left foot of the Elvis Presley float."

"But I'll bet Stolarz has removed them by now," Joe put in.

"That's another thing," Tomas interrupted. "Suppose you're right about all this. What makes you think Mr. Stolarz is behind it? Just because stuff is hidden in a warehouse belonging to him doesn't mean he knows anything about it."

"Okay, okay," Joe said impatiently. "But will you at least check this out? I mean, maybe it is a reason Billy Barta was killed."

Tomas snorted. "Boy, you're really stretchin'

it. What do you boys think you are—detectives or somethin'?"

Joe shot Frank a wry look.

"You mean the reason you were staking Billy out has nothing to do with stolen technology?" Joe challenged.

"Nuh-uh," Tomas said, shaking his head. "And stop it right there because you aren't gettin' anything more out of me. The reason why Billy Barta was under surveillance is confidential." He picked up the card and the circuit board and came around the edge of his desk, heading for the door. "Dumont!" he shouted into the hallway. "Get in here!"

A lanky young officer came in. "Yes, sir?" he said.

"Make sure these three don't go anywhere while I'm gone." Turning to Frank, Joe, and Vanessa, he added, "I'm going to pay Mr. Stolarz a visit, then have our experts examine these."

"You won't be sorry, Captain Tomas," Joe said sincerely.

"I'd better not be," the captain said, his expression darkening. "I hate wastin' time, y'understand? Meantime, you're gonna stay here until I personally release you."

"No problem," Frank said, nodding.

"Let's hope not," Tomas warned. "Best y'all can hope for is that you're material witnesses to a felony—the theft of this here circuitry. Worst case, you and the young lady are going to join your brother in jail, after I arrest y'all."

"For what?" Joe asked.

"Burglarizin' Mr. Stolarz's warehouse—that's what." And with that, he walked out of the room, locking the door behind him.

Chapter

9

JOE, FRANK, AND VANESSA stood staring at the door for an incredibly long time. "It's like a bad dream!" Vanessa finally said, her voice barely a whisper.

"Don't worry, Vanessa," Joe told her. "When Tomas finds out what's on that flash memory card and circuit board, we'll be home free."

"I don't know," Frank said, scowling. "There's something strange about it all. Billy Barta was hiding something from Stolarz, remember. At least, he didn't want to use Stolarz's phones for his 'personal business.' And what about the death of Antoine LeMieux? Does his mother know more than she's telling us?"

"She sure acts like she does," Vanessa said. "But then again, that's her business."

"She's been pretty good at predicting the future so far," Joe said.

Frank had to smile. "This is the same guy who wouldn't be caught dead having his fortune told," he said drily.

"It's not funny, Frank," Joe said. "We went off the road in the fog. We got away from Stolarz's that first time by diving into the river on a clear night. The Devil float, Elvis being the King..."

Frank sighed. "The question is, is that all just fortune-telling, or is she in on what's happening? We'd better keep an eye on her. As soon as Tomas springs us, that is."

Captain Tomas was gone for almost two hours. When he opened the door and walked in, he was not smiling. In fact, he was steaming mad.

"All right, you kids," he began. "I've had enough. If you're tryin' to prove your brother is innocent," he said to Frank, "this is no way to go about it."

"I don't know what you're talking about, sir," Frank said, shaking his head in frustration.

"Yeah," Joe put in. "Didn't you see what was on that circuitry?"

"I saw, all right," Tomas told them. "That circuit board contained a very sophisticated computer chip—one that isn't supposed to leave the country, if you catch my drift."

"Did you ask Stolarz what it was doing in his warehouse?" Joe demanded.

"I did," Tomas said, turning to him. "He says he never had anything like it in there. I had my men do a search of the premises, and they didn't turn up a thing."

"Nothing on the Elvis float?" Frank asked, amazed.

"Nothin'," Tomas said gravely.

"Well, didn't you at least bring Stolarz in for questioning?" Joe asked.

"No, I did not. Mr. Stolarz is an upstandin' businessman in this city," Tomas spat out. "I've about lost my patience with you. I don't know where you got this circuit board, but I'm going to hang on to it for a while."

Joe stood staring at the detective, his eyes wide with fury. Frank put a restraining hand on his brother's arm.

But the officer's expression softened. "All right," he said to Joe. "I'm going to let you out of here one more time. If I could arrange it, you'd be in front of a judge right now. But since Mr. Stolarz refused to press charges for breakin' an' enterin'—even though you confessed it—my hands are tied."

"He isn't going to press charges?" Frank asked, stunned.

"Nope. In fact, he says y'all were never even there. All you've got is a circuit board you could have picked up anywhere and a blank flash memory card."

"Blank?" Frank asked.

"It was blank when we ran it on our in-house computer. You can keep it, because it's no good to me." Tomas flipped it over to him. "If you kids can come up with something to prove Joe is innocent, I'd be glad to listen, but you've got to stop messin' with me. You give me any more trouble and I'll bring you in for obstruction of justice."

Frank bit his lip to keep his anger in check. "There was something on that card, Captain," he said. "It was software for a sophisticated weapons guidance system. And we *did* find it in Stolarz's warehouse, no matter what Stolarz told you."

"All right," Tomas said, shaking his head. "I'll keep my eyes open, okay? That's all I'm promisin'. Now get out of here, and don't come back unless you've got real proof. But whatever you do—don't leave town."

Outside, the Hardys and Vanessa tried to make sense of what had just happened. "Could we have accidentally erased the flash memory card when we ran it at Decoders?" Joe asked.

"Or maybe the police accidentally erased it," Vanessa suggested.

"It may even have erased itself—a kind of fail-safe device in case too many people try to access it in too short a time." Frank shrugged.

"What a bad break, though." Vanessa sighed. "Well, it looks like we're back to square one. What do we do now? Head back to Madame LeMieux's?"

"No," Frank said. "Stolarz is where the action is. He's up to something illegal for sure."

"How do you know?" Vanessa asked. "Like Tomas said, maybe he didn't know the stuff was in his warehouse."

"He knew," Joe said. "If he didn't, he would have had us charged with breaking and entering, instead of denying we were there."

"Exactly," Frank said. "I say we follow Mr. Stolarz wherever he goes. There's a pay phone at the corner." He fished in his pocket for change. "I'll call to find out if he's at work."

While Joe and Vanessa went to a convenience store and stocked up on junk food to sustain them during their stakeout, Frank dialed the warehouse. "Is Mr. Stolarz in?"

"Who may I say is calling?" said the receptionist.

"The American International Commerce Institute," Frank answered, making up the name.

There was a short silence while the receptionist repeated what he'd said to someone nearby. "Mr. Stolarz is in a meeting. May I have him call you back?"

"I'll try again later," Frank said. "About what time will his meeting be over?"

"He could be there all day," said the receptionist.

Frank hung up just as Joe and Vanessa returned, loaded down with potato chips, juices, pretzels, and other assorted goodies. "It could be a long, boring afternoon," Frank told them. "Stolarz is in a meeting."

"I don't know," Vanessa replied with a sly smile. "Knowing you two and your ability to attract trouble, something tells me it isn't going to be boring at all."

Vanessa was wrong. The junk food and juices were running out, and the sun was setting by the time Stolarz finally left the warehouse, got into his car, and headed out of the lot.

"Finally!" Joe said, straightening up in his seat.

"Here we go, guys," Frank said, starting the engine. "Let's hope this turns out to be worth the wait."

Stolarz drove down North Peters Street and stopped at the light at Canal. Frank saw him look in his rearview mirror, and hoped they hadn't been spotted.

But as soon as Stolarz got moving again, it became apparent that he knew he was being followed. He took a right on Canal, then another right onto Chartres. His wheels burned rubber as Frank raced to keep up.

Stolarz proceeded to lead them on a hair-raising chase up and down the streets of the French Quarter. "Whoa, baby!" Joe yelled as they careened around a corner.

"Hold on to your hats, guys!" Frank said, executing a quick one-eighty to stay with Stolarz's black coupe. The two cars raced back toward Canal Street. There, Stolarz ran a yellow light that then turned red, and crosstown traffic blocked the Hardys' way.

"Rats!" Frank shouted, banging the wheel in frustration. "We might as well go home for the night," Joe said. "We can try again tomorrow."

When they pulled into Aunt Violet's driveway, Catlin was waiting for them with the cordless phone. "It's All-Night Al," she said, handing Joe the phone. "He wants to talk to you."

Joe took the phone and said, "Hi, Al. What's up?"

Al's voice was a hoarse whisper, full of annoyance. "I'm on the corner of Rigaudin and Beauregard," he said. "I want you here twenty minutes ago. And you better leave the girls at home this time. This neighborhood could give *bad* a bad name." He hung up without waiting for a reply from Joe.

"Sounds urgent," Joe said as Frank ran to the car for a street map. On the porch, they figured out how to get where they were going. Then they got into their rental car and set off into the darkened, misty streets of New Orleans.

Joe drove and Frank tried to follow the map. They got lost twice. It was twenty minutes later when they finally found themselves on a back street in a rundown neighborhood near the river. They parked the car and advanced slowly toward the desolate corner where Al had said he'd meet them.

Frank went first, with Joe bringing up the rear. He checked over his shoulder to make sure they weren't being followed. The storefronts were all boarded up, and the deserted street was filled with litter and rubble. All but one of the street lamps had been shattered, probably by vandals, Joe thought.

He felt a chill creep slowly up his spine as he stared ahead of him at Frank's back. Something was wrong—it was too quiet. Twice, he sensed someone following them. But each time he turned around, there was no one there. So, he kept walking.

They were passing a junked car when Joe felt a hand close over his mouth. Even though his instincts were on the alert, it took him completely by surprise.

Before he could strike back, a pair of iron-strong hands knocked him off balance and dragged him into an alleyway.

Chapter

10

"DON'T MAKE A SOUND!"

Joe's eyes widened as he was spun around and found himself staring into the steely eyes of All-Night Al.

Al signaled for Joe to wait by pointing to his watch. Seconds later, Joe realized why. Frank, who had been walking twenty or so feet ahead of Joe, came back around the corner of the alley, looking for him.

"Joe!" Frank whispered. "Oh, there you are. Hi, Al."

"Shhh!" Al said, holding a finger to his lips. He beckoned for them to follow him to the back of the alley.

It was pitch-dark away from the street, but

clearly Al wanted it that way. He dusted off the top of an old milk crate before sitting down on it.

"I been checkin' up on you boys," he said, his voice barely a whisper. "Looks like your daddy's a big man in Bayport, and I understand you two are in the business yourselves. So I thought I'd see what I could do to help you out. I was followin' you earlier this evenin' while you were tailin' Stolarz. You lost him, but I didn't."

"All right, Al!" Frank said, making a triumphant fist.

"So where is Stolarz?" Joe asked.

"Across the street, four buildings down," Al replied. "In a little apartment at the back of an alley just like this one. He rang the bell, and a big fella answered the door. They're in there now. You can see through the window, but you've got to get right next to the wall to hear anything. And at my age, I don't go no closer than this. So you're on your own. Good luck. I got my money ridin' on you." Tipping an imaginary hat to them, Al walked off down the alley.

"Can you believe that guy?" Joe asked. "I thought I was going to die!"

"The night isn't over," Frank warned him.

Joe looked out at the street, glistening yellow in the light of the one remaining street lamp. "Foggy night, too," he grumbled as they headed toward the street. "Not a good sign."

"Never mind, Joe," Frank said with a smile. "This is our big break. I can feel it in my bones."

They crossed the street, ducked into the alley All-Night Al had pointed out, and walked silently to the very back of it. The alley led between two buildings to a garage. Behind the building on the left was a small backyard with a large weeping willow in the center. In the rear wall of the building was a door with two steps leading up to it, which gave onto an apartment. To the right of the door, about twenty feet from the tree, was a large open window. Through it, they could see Stolarz pacing, checking his watch impatiently.

A black cat howled from the top of a chain link fence at the rear of the trash-filled backyard. Both Frank and Joe jumped reflexively, taking cover behind the trunk of the tree. The cat jumped down and disappeared from view.

"I wonder if we missed anything important," Joe said as they both peeked at the window again.

At that moment someone else walked into the room—a large man, wearing a trench coat and a wide-brimmed hat.

"The foreman from Stolarz's warehouse!" Frank whispered.

Stolarz said something to the foreman, but it was impossible to hear him. Both brothers crept under the window. The light above the rear door shone right on them. They had to hope no one else came down the alleyway.

Joe could hear his heart pounding. It amazed him that the men inside couldn't hear it, too.

And then, a car engine sounded in the distance. "Get out there, Ralph," Joe heard Stolarz tell his foreman.

Looking up, Joe saw the apartment door not six feet from where they were crouching. Was this the door the foreman would use? Should they make a run for it back to the tree?

By the time Joe had decided, it was too late. In that moment of hesitation, the door swung open and the foreman stepped outside. He drew his unbuttoned trench coat around him and tilted his hat lower down on his head. Joe and Frank both held their breath, knowing that if he turned their way, they were finished.

But the foreman turned to his right, heading for the alleyway, where the sound of the car's engine grew louder, then stopped. The foreman drew a gun from his trench coat, then disappeared around the corner of the building.

Once he had his back to them, Frank and Joe nodded silently to each other, then made for the tree.

Joe heard the car door open and shut. Inside the apartment, Stolarz walked to the window and stared out suspiciously, then drew the shade down. The Hardys could see his backlit shadow now, but that was all.

The sound of footsteps reached them. Joe's keen ears told him that only one person was returning. The foreman strode back down the alley and rounded the corner of the building—alone. His trench coat was buttoned now, and the collar was up high. The hat was pulled down low, so that Joe couldn't make out his face. No shots had been fired, but the car had not been driven away.

The man walked slowly, deliberately, unlike the way he'd gone down the alley before, when he'd seemed in a great hurry.

The foreman paused when he reached the rear door, then entered the apartment. And now, through the shade, the Hardys could see the shadows of the two men inside. They seemed to be arguing. Frank tilted his head toward the window to signal Joe, and seconds later they were crouched under it again.

"I'll go keep an eye on the alley," Frank whispered. "In case the driver of the car decides to join them." He crept over to the corner of the building.

Still underneath the window, Joe strained hard to listen. "What about those kids?" he heard Stolarz ask.

"Don't worry," the other man said in a hoarse, throaty whisper. "If they come close again, I'll take care of them."

97

"You let them get away!" Stolarz said, his voice rising.

"I'm tellin' you, I can handle them."

Joe's throat was dry. Had the foreman been the one who'd pushed him off the streetcar?

"Don't mess around," Stolarz said. "Do them now—like you did Billy. I can't take any chances."

"You're already takin' chances by dealin' with *me*."

"All right," Stolarz said, a note coming into his voice that sounded somewhat pleading. "What do you want?"

"Full partnership," said the other man, "including Billy's share."

"What?" Stolarz gasped. "I've been payin' you off since the start. That's enough!"

"Not anymore, Stolarz. I've got the piece of hardware Billy stole from you. Without that interface to attach the guidance software to the missile itself, your circuit boards and flash memory cards won't be much good to whoever you're sellin' them to."

"Billy told you all that?" Stolarz gasped.

"We were partners," the other man said. "Until he decided to cut my share of the profits. Don't make the mistake he did. You could end up the same way."

"You wouldn't dare!" Stolarz said. "Without me, you couldn't sell any of this stuff! I'm the one who bought it all on the black market! I'm the one who contacted the customers abroad. They deal only with me!"

"True," said the big man in the trench coat. "But *you've* got to deal with *me*." He laughed menacingly.

"Why, I oughta—" Stolarz began.

"What are you going to do—call the police?"

"All right," Stolarz said grudgingly. "Full partners."

Just then, the black cat who had startled them before leapt off a garbage can, sending the lid clattering to the ground. The shadows in the window turned sharply.

"What was that?" Stolarz gasped.

"Let's go see," said the other man. Through the shade, the Hardys saw his silhouette draw a gun.

"Let's get out of here!" Frank whispered. Without looking behind them, they raced down the alley, passing the car they'd heard on their way.

Shots rang out as Frank reached the street. Joe saw his brother's hand fly up to his face. Then Frank rounded the front of the building with Joe right behind him.

Frank got to their car first, and yanked open the passenger door. Joe had the keys in his hand. He gunned the engine and was halfway down the street by the time the bullets started flying again.

Joe screeched around the corner and kept going until he felt sure that no one was following.

"That was a close one, huh, Frank?"

Frank didn't answer. Joe turned to see why not—then hit the brakes. Frank's face was covered with blood!

Chapter

11

"FRANK! ARE YOU ALL RIGHT?" Joe pulled the car over, and quickly ripped off a shirtsleeve to wipe the blood from his brother's face. Much to his relief, he saw that the cut on Frank's forehead was only superficial. "You must have been grazed by a bullet," he said, giving Frank an encouraging smile. "Look at the bright side—another inch to the right and we wouldn't be sitting here chatting like this."

"What a way with words you've got," Frank groused.

"Do you want to go to a hospital?" Joe asked.

"Nah," Frank said, closing his eyes. "Just head back to Violet's. I need to lie down, but I'll be all right."

Joe wound his sleeve around Frank's head, tying it tightly to stop the bleeding. Then he started the car and headed for the Garden District.

The others were shocked when they saw Frank stumble out of the car with a bloody bandage on his head. It was now after ten, but Aunt Violet woke up a neighbor who was a doctor, and he came over and gave Frank four stitches.

When it was all over, Frank and Joe told them the whole story. Just as they finished, Joe heard the sound of a car pulling into the driveway. All-Night Al got out of it.

"Evenin', Violet," he said, coming up the front steps of the veranda. "You're lookin' lovely in the moonlight."

"Al, you never change," Violet replied.

"Evenin', everybody," Al said, straightening up. "You fellas okay? I was in the neighborhood and thought I'd find out what happened to the two of you."

"Frank caught a ricochet on the forehead," Joe told him, then filled Al in on their adventure, and on what they'd heard.

Al frowned. "Sounds like Stolarz is up to his ears in dirty business," he said. "But he's a big man in town and Tomas knows it. It isn't going to be easy to get the police to move against him. What about the other man?"

"We didn't actually see his face," Frank pointed out.

"What do you mean, Frank?" Joe asked. "We saw the foreman go out of there. Then he went back in, and he and Stolarz had their argument."

"Right," Frank agreed. "But that doesn't explain the car we heard stopping in the alley. It could have been a third man who came back into the apartment, dressed the same as the foreman." He shook his head, perplexed. "Oh, well. I guess we've got to move on what we know. How can we find out the foreman's last name, and where he lives?"

"I can do that for you," Al volunteered. "I've got connections in this town. For now, get yourselves some sleep. Y'all look like you need it. I'll call you in the mornin'."

By the time the boys made it down to breakfast the next morning, it was nine o'clock. The smell of bacon frying filled the house, and Catlin and Vanessa were sitting in front of the remains of their meal.

"Well!" Vanessa said, her eyes widening as the Hardys walked in. "You certainly look a lot better than you did last night, Frank."

"I feel a lot better," Frank said, sitting down.

"Al called about an hour ago," Catlin told them. "He gave me the foreman's name and address." She handed Frank a piece of paper.

"Ralph Redfern," he read. "Ten Forty-six Beauregard. Hey, Joe, that's the house we were at last night."

"So they were meeting at his place!" Joe said excitedly. "Frank, we ought to go back there. Redfern should be at work now. Maybe we can find something."

"Like the strongbox with the computer boards and flash memory cards?" Frank asked. "It's a shot. After all, we know that it wasn't at Stolarz's warehouse when Tomas went over there to look for it."

"One other thing," Catlin interrupted. "Al says he heard through his contacts that Tomas has convinced the DA to bring murder charges against Joe. He said you'd better hurry up and find some hard evidence fast."

Frank and Joe exchanged worried glances. "Well, Joe," Frank said as Violet came out with their breakfasts of bacon and eggs, "let's eat up quick and get over there."

"What about Catlin and me?" Vanessa asked.

"Hmmm," Frank said thoughtfully. "Why don't you guys take a little drive downtown. Go by Billy Barta's place and see what the surveillance looks like. Maybe we can try getting in there later today."

"Deal," Vanessa said. "Where should we meet?"

"How about Quatraine's on Chartres Street for lunch?" Catlin suggested.

"Okay," Joe said. They all got up to go.

"Hold on a minute!" Aunt Violet called, coming in from the kitchen and putting her hands on her blue-jeaned hips. "I'm tired of hangin' around here worryin'."

"We'll call at noon," Joe promised her. "And don't worry, Aunt Violet—we'll take good care of the girls."

"Hmmm," Violet said dubiously. "Better than you did your brother, I hope."

Redfern's apartment was deserted, as was the whole street. The boys got in through the window near the willow tree, but were disappointed to find the place empty. There wasn't even a stick of furniture inside.

"Obviously, the guy doesn't really live here," Joe said.

"This must be just a cover," Frank replied. "Maybe this is where Stolarz meets his foreign clients, too."

"We ought to tell Tomas about it," Joe suggested. "Maybe he can have it staked out."

Frank frowned. "Tomas doesn't believe a word we've been telling him, don't you get it, Joe? He's convinced Stolarz is innocent. I guess I would be, too, if I were him. Stolarz has been pretty good about covering his tracks."

"Oh, well. Time to go meet Vanessa and Catlin," Joe said, checking his watch.

They drove to the French Quarter and found Quatraine's, where Vanessa and Catlin were waiting for them. "Billy's place is all cordoned off," Vanessa told them after they'd called Aunt Violet to report that they were all still in one piece. "I don't see how we can get in there."

"Maybe we can't," Frank said. "But I know one place I definitely want to go back to—Denise LeMieux's. I want to get another look at her son Antoine's room. He was close friends with Billy Barta. And his mother's kept his room exactly as it was. I've got a hunch we may find something there, if we look hard enough."

"What are you all doin' back here?" Denise LeMieux stood in her doorway, eyeing them suspiciously.

"If you don't mind, ma'am," Frank said, "we'd like to have another look at Antoine's room."

"You seen it already," she said.

"Please," Joe interjected. "We may have missed something, and the police are going to arrest me for murdering Billy Barta unless I can find some evidence to clear myself."

Madame LeMieux hesitated, the lines of grief in her face seeming to grow even deeper. Then she silently beckoned them inside and led them back to the little cubicle she had turned into a shrine to her son. She hovered at the door and watched.

"Say, how do you do your predictions?" Joe asked her as they looked around. "They're unbelievably accurate."

Madame LeMieux smiled mysteriously. "The cards never lie," she said simply. "Although they don't always tell me everything. They didn't say you would come back here."

"We weren't planning on it," Frank said.

"What's this?" Vanessa asked, holding up a file folder she'd found in the desk drawer. It was labeled Xanadu.

"Xanadu—it's a Mardi Gras krewe," Madame LeMieux explained. "The krewes design the floats and run them in the parade. That's how Antoine got mixed up with Billy in the first place. They was both in Xanadu."

Frank examined the contents of the folder. There were blueprints for floats and lists of members, including Billy Barta. Nothing helpful, though.

"Hey, look at this, you guys," Catlin said suddenly. She had been searching behind some photos on a bookshelf, and now held up a key on a keychain that would float.

Frank took the key and looked at it. The label on the chain read Pontchartrain Belle.

"That's Billy's boat," Madame LeMieux told

them. "Don't know why he gave Antoine a key for it."

"Do you mind if we hang on to this?" Frank asked. "I'd like to check it out. We might find something there."

"Go ahead," Madame LeMieux said with a shrug.

The Hardys, Vanessa, and Catlin left the fortune-teller's shop, excited. "All we need now," Catlin said, "is to find out where Billy's boat is berthed."

"Somewhere on Lake Pontchartrain, I'll bet," Vanessa said.

"But it's a big lake," Frank commented. "We could spend days looking. But maybe there's something in Billy's place that would tell us where it is."

"You heard the girls," Joe said dryly, "the whole place is cordoned off."

"I don't see that we have a choice," Frank said. "Besides, I've got an idea. . . ."

Half an hour later they were all strolling down the street toward Billy Barta's apartment. Frank walked ahead with Catlin and Vanessa. Joe trailed about fifty feet behind.

The alley that led back to Billy's apartment was indeed cordoned off. In front, on the street, two police stood idly passing the time, watching tourists stroll by on this beautiful, sunny day.

Across the street an artist sat on a stool and painted while all around her vendors hawked souvenirs.

Frank and the girls, with the cameras, guidebooks, and sunglasses they'd just bought, looked for all the world like three tourists.

"Excuse me," Catlin said to one of the police. "Is this where the Voodoo Museum is?"

"Uh, no, ma'am," the officer said. "It's on Bourbon."

"Where's that?" Catlin asked, unfolding a large map. While the officer helped her hold up the map, fighting the breeze that kept blowing it around, Vanessa and Frank approached the other officer.

"We're looking for St. Louis Cemetery," they told him.

"St. Louis one, two, or three?" the man asked.

Just as they'd planned, Frank and Vanessa opened up their enormous map and asked the officer for help reading it. While they did this, Joe slipped under the yellow police tape unnoticed. He walked through the brick archway, quickly moving out of sight, figuring that he had only a few minutes at most. He had to work fast. Luckily, there was no third officer in the rear of the alley to guard the door of the apartment itself. Joe broke the seal on the door and took out his lock pick. But the lock was old and rusty, and Joe grumbled in frustration as he tried to get it to move. Finally he succeeded, but he'd eaten up precious time in the process.

Once inside, he quickly moved toward Billy's desk. He knew that the police would have removed any hard evidence they'd found. But Joe was looking for one thing only—the location of Billy's boat. He searched frantically through the messy pile of bills, credit card receipts, and phone messages.

Finally he found what he needed—a receipt for diesel fuel. What other reason could Billy have for buying diesel fuel than to fill his boat's tank? And if they knew where he bought his fuel, maybe they could trace the boat from there. Joe checked his watch again. He'd been in the apartment for almost five minutes, much longer than he'd meant to stay. Stuffing the receipt into his pocket, he headed for the door, reached for the knob, and pulled it toward him.

There, staring at him, was one of the two police officers from out front. Before Joe could move a muscle, the officer had his gun drawn and was pointing it straight at Joe's head!

Chapter

12

"OFFICER, QUICK!" JOE SAID, thinking on his feet. "In the back room—there's another body!"

"Another body!" The young officer didn't stop to think, but ran for the back room. As soon as he turned the corner, Joe raced out of the apartment and down the alley.

Just as he reached the street, he heard a whistle behind him. "Stop that kid!" the officer shouted to his partner.

The other man got off to a slow start because Frank and the girls made it as hard as they could for him to get around them. Meanwhile, Joe took off down the street, rounding the first corner and ducking into an alley until the two police had gone by. Then he doubled back and headed for the rented car, which was parked nearby.

Frank and the girls showed up at the same moment. Joe hit the gas and tore off down the street. "Whew," Frank said, letting out a sigh of relief when they'd gotten away.

"I nearly dropped dead when that officer met me at the door!"

"Slow down, Joe," Vanessa warned. "You don't want to get us pulled over for speeding."

"You got that right," Joe agreed, taking his foot off the accelerator.

"In fact," Frank added, "we'd better stay out of sight of all police from now on. They got a good look at us, and they're likely to come for us once Tomas puts two and two together."

"Hey, I found what we were looking for," Joe said, fishing out the receipt for diesel fuel. "Handy Andy's Pump 'n' Go. It must be somewhere on Lake Pontchartrain."

"Should be easy enough to find out," Frank said.

"Yup," Joe replied. "Hopefully, whoever works there will be able to point us to Billy's boat."

As soon as they got back to Aunt Violet's, Vanessa called Handy Andy and got directions. Meanwhile, Catlin told her aunt what they'd been up to while the Hardys sat down on the front porch to talk things over.

"So where are we?" Frank asked.

"Well, we know Stolarz is in the business of smuggling missile technology to foreign interests, whoever they are."

"Go on," Frank said.

"And we know his partner is his foreman, Redfern," Joe continued. "What's more, they're fighting."

"But, Joe, we don't know for certain that it was Redfern in there with Stolarz."

"Who else could it have been?"

"Think, Joe," Frank told him. "After Redfern went outside, Stolarz put the shades down, and then we saw only shadows."

"Well, if Redfern wasn't in there, where did he go? Wouldn't he have been in the car when we came running out? Why didn't he come after us?"

"It probably was Redfern," Frank admitted. "All I'm saying is, we don't know for sure. We do know Redfern's in on it, though."

"It does seem kind of weird for a guy like Stolarz to be partners with his foreman," Joe mused.

"You never know," Frank pointed out. Absentmindedly, he fished the flash memory card out of his shirt pocket and looked at it. "I've also been wondering how the data on this got wiped out."

"Well, like we said before," Joe began. "Either Tomas's experts erased it accidentally, or the guy at Decoders messed it up while he was taking it off the machine—"

"Wait a second!" Frank gasped, standing up and staring intently at the card. "Check this out, Joe."

"Looks fine to me," Joe said.

"That's just it!" Frank said excitedly. "The card I gave Tomas was all scratched up."

"You mean—"

"This isn't the same card I gave Tomas," Frank said. "He said he went over to Stolarz's warehouse. He probably took it with him. What if Stolarz switched it?"

"Yeah," Joe said, nodding. "That would explain why Tomas thought our card was a blank."

Vanessa came out onto the porch. "I got the directions," she said, plopping down on a wicker armchair. "But Handy Andy says he's closing in half an hour. We'll never make it."

"We can try," Frank said. "Come on, Joe. Let's get a move on. Vanessa, you and Catlin stay here—if Tomas sends his men out to arrest Joe, tell him we skipped town."

"Oooh!" Vanessa said, raising her eyebrows. "That's going to make him so mad!"

Joe and Frank set off for Lake Pontchartrain. It was enormous, and Joe imagined that it must once have been wild and unspoiled. Now it had become polluted from overuse. Hundreds of boats bobbed in its waters, and Joe smelled petroleum and rotting vegetation through the open car window.

As it turned out, Handy Andy's was on the far side of the lake in a quiet area. Handy Andy himself was old and nearly toothless, with leathery, wrinkled skin and bright blue eyes. When Frank and Joe found him, he was on his back with a wrench, working on the underside of a fuel truck.

"*Pontchartrain Belle?*" he repeated when Frank told him the name of the boat they were looking for. "Oh, yeah, she's out there at anchor. Been there for over a week, and ain't nobody gone to see her."

"Her owner's dead," Frank explained. "The family asked us to come out here and have a look at her."

"That handsome young fella? Dead?" Handy Andy clucked his tongue sorrowfully. "How d'ye like that?" He sighed deeply. "Well, you don't need my permission t' go out to his boat. Y'all can borrow the skiff to get out there, long as you return it."

"Thanks, Andy," Frank said.

"Boat's about a quarter knot out yonder," Andy said, pointing due west. "You can't miss her."

"Much obliged," Joe said, reaching for his wallet.

"Oh, no, I don't want no money," Andy told

him, waving away the offer. "What I'm gonna do with it at my age, anyhow?"

"Have you ever thought of retiring?" Frank asked him as they picked up a pair of oars for the skiff.

"Me? Retire?" the old man scoffed. "No, sonny, I like my life just like it is. Honest work's what keeps a body alive, y'know."

"Too bad Billy didn't believe that," Joe said under his breath.

Frank and Joe waved goodbye to Handy Andy and rowed out to Billy Barta's boat, a twenty-four-foot cabin cruiser that had seen better days. The boys tied up the dinghy, clambered on board the boat, and searched it thoroughly. In the polished wood map box in the cabin Joe found a chart that he showed Frank.

"Navigational," Frank remarked, scanning the chart. "It pinpoints a spot about fifteen miles out into the Gulf. I wonder what it means."

"If Billy was a part of Stolarz's smuggling ring," Joe ventured, "then maybe this is where they met their foreign customers. It's outside the twelve-mile limit, in international waters. The New Orleans police couldn't touch them there. Neither could the Coast Guard."

"I bet that's it." Frank turned the chart over. "Hey, look here—another chart, with directions!"

Joe read the directions out loud. " 'Follow shoreline to marker oh-seven-four-oh. Turn inland two and one quarter knots, enter Bayou St. Cloud, one-half knot to cabin.' Paydirt, Frank!"

"Let's go find that cabin," Frank said. "If the police haven't searched it, maybe we'll find the evidence we need to clear you."

"You mean, take Billy's boat?" Joe asked.

"Billy won't mind," Frank pointed out.

"True," Joe acknowledged. "But what about Handy Andy's skiff?"

"We'll get it back to him later," Frank said. "Come on, Joe, start her up. This could be the break we've been looking for."

The boys inserted the key they'd found at Antoine's, revved up the engine, and cast off, heading out toward the narrow entrance to the Gulf of Mexico. Once out on the open water, they turned westward, hugging the coast, past the mouth of the Mississippi.

The trip took almost two hours. Frank and Joe made several wrong turns up bayous that ended in confusing mazes before they found themselves on the swampy slough called Bayou St. Cloud.

Here the towering live oaks dripping with Spanish moss all but blocked out the sun. Alligators lazed along the banks of the bayou and wading birds fished in the silence, broken only by the motor of the *Pontchartrain Belle*.

"A little off the beaten track, huh?' Joe remarked.

Ten minutes later they saw the little cabin up

ahead. It sat on the banks of the bayou, with a tumbledown dock in front of it and a rutted dirt road leading off into the trees behind it. In the distance, the road passed what looked like an old store.

Frank killed the engine and the boat glided slowly toward the dock. Joe tied her up, and then they hopped out and walked to the shack. "I sure hope nobody's home," Joe said under his breath.

"Me, too," Frank agreed. He crept up to the window, which was nothing more than a hole in the wall with a plastic shade drawn down on the inside. Frank silently pushed it aside and looked in. The cabin was dark, but clearly empty.

Frank and Joe went around to the creaky wooden door, pushed it open, and stepped inside. There wasn't a thing inside of interest. A quick once-over revealed only a table, a few chairs, and some fishing gear.

"This sure isn't the kind of place Billy would have lived in," Joe said, carefully stepping over the old floorboards. "I guess whoever owns it just used it for stowing fishing stuff. If there was ever anything important here, somebody else must have gotten rid of it."

"Too bad," Frank agreed. "Come on, let's get out of here. It's going to take us a couple of hours to get back."

It was getting dark now, but having memorized their route, they made the return trip without incident. It was after seven o'clock when Frank pulled up to the buoy where they'd first found the boat. While he idled the motor, Joe tied the *Pontchartrain Belle* to the buoy, then went back down to join Frank in the cabin.

"I hear a boat cruising around out there," Joe remarked. "But I don't see any running lights. Weird, huh?"

Frank frowned, cut the engine, and listened. The other boat's motor was quite close. "Joe, are you thinking what I'm thinking?" he asked.

"Probably," Joe replied.

"Come on," Frank said. But before they could scramble onto the deck, something clattered down into the cabin and rolled under the control panel. Frank followed the object—and what he saw made his eyes nearly pop out of his head.

"A grenade!" he shouted. "Quick, Joe—bail out!"

Chapter

13

JOE AND FRANK CLAMBERED up the three steps to the deck and flung themselves in the murky lake. The explosion came just as Frank hit the water. The shock wave sent him reeling.

When he finally came to the surface, the fireball that had been Billy Barta's boat was still mushrooming skyward, and debris was falling all around him—planks, shattered pieces of metal, broken glass. Frank dove again to avoid being hit.

The next time he came up for air, he heard the engine of the other boat running full, retreating into the darkness. Handy Andy's dinghy floated a little way off, but the *Pontchartrain Belle* was demolished. Frank dragged himself onto the dinghy. He was covered with muck and seaweed and worried sick about Joe.

Then a mud-coated monster rose out of the lake and swam toward Frank. "Joe!" Frank shouted, leaning over to pull his brother on board. "You made it!"

"Do I look as gross as you do?" Joe asked, plopping down on the seat next to Frank. "Hey, do you get the idea that someone wants to get rid of us?"

Frank didn't have to answer.

"I think we're safe now," Joe said. "I heard a boat pull away. Besides, if I'd thrown a grenade, I wouldn't hang around to pick up the pieces."

They rowed back to shore, listening to the moaning of distant sirens. Just as they reached the dock, two police cars came careening along the lakeside road. The officers took down Frank and Joe's versions of what had happened, but insisted that they accompany them to police headquarters.

As they sat in the back of the squad car, Frank turned to Joe. "What are you thinking about?"

"I'm wondering what Tomas is going to say when he finds out we commandeered Billy Barta's boat and got it blown sky-high?"

Tomas was furious. "That boat was potential state's evidence!" he roared as the boys sat in his office. They had been allowed to shower and change into some surplus clothing. But they were now in more trouble than ever.

"No All-Night Al's going to spring you this time," Tomas said, scowling.

"Does that mean you're arresting us?" Joe asked.

"That's right," Tomas said. "Consider your rights read to you. I got you for criminal trespass, tamperin' with evidence, and suspicion of murder in the Billy Barta case."

"Doesn't it mean anything to you, Captain," Frank ventured, "that someone tried to blow us up out on the lake?"

"I only have your word for that," Tomas said. "How do I know y'all didn't blow up that boat yourselves so whatever evidence was on it would disappear?"

Frank sighed and shook his head. There was no way they were going to get another chance to clear Joe now. "Do we at least get to make a phone call?"

Tomas frowned, then shoved the phone across the desk at Frank. "Make it quick."

Frank called Aunt Violet and told her what had happened. "What?" Violet gasped in disbelief. "He can't blame you for blowin' up that boat."

"That's just what he's doing," Frank told her grimly.

"Well, you sit tight," she told him. "I know somebody who may be able to help."

Frank hung up only a little more hopeful than he'd been before. Tomas then led them down to the lockup. "Keep an eye on these two," he told the guard in the hallway. "They've got a way of squirmin' out of things."

Frank and Joe settled in to wait—for what, they didn't know. But it was only an hour or so later when the door of their cell was opened again and they were led back upstairs to the office of Captain Tomas.

"Seems you fellas have friends in high places. I got a message from the Chief of the NOPD himself, orderin' me to let you two loose. I'll tell you this, though—the first whiff I get of you bein' in trouble again—not even the President of the United States'll be able to get you sprung. Now get out of here, y' hear?"

He slammed his fist down on his desk, sending papers flying in all directions. Frank and Joe didn't help him pick up the mess.

As Frank reached the doorway, something made him pause—a photograph on the wall to the right of the door frame. It was a picture of Tomas, holding up a large fish, standing in front of a cabin with a little dock.

"I said get out!" Tomas roared.

Frank scooted out, right behind Joe, his heart racing. He was almost positive he'd seen the cabin in the photo somewhere before.

"We've got to get back into Tomas's office and check out that picture," Frank told Joe over breakfast the next morning.

"Oh, no, you don't," Violet said firmly, handing out seconds of waffles and sausage. "Chief Nolan was very gracious to let you boys out of there—he's an ol' friend, y' know. But I don't want him regretting his decision.

"I'm afraid you boys are in danger of exhausting all the goodwill I've built up over the years," Violet said with a shake of her head. "Please stay here from now on. Let the police do their jobs—I'm sure you'll be cleared eventually."

"I wish I was as sure as you, Aunt Violet," Frank said. "But I'm afraid this case is different from most. I saw something in Tomas's office last night that changes everything, but we've got to go back to be sure."

"Oh, no, you don't," Vanessa said. "You guys go in there, and the next thing you know we'll be visiting you in jail."

"Why don't you let All-Night Al handle this for you?" Aunt Violet suggested.

"Sorry, Aunt Violet," Frank said. "Only Joe and I will be able to make sense of this photograph. Besides, I've got a plan to get us in and out without being noticed."

Aunt Violet cocked an eyebrow. "How intriguing," she said, pulling up a chair. "Now, this I'd like to hear."

Right about noon Frank and Joe showed up at NOPD Headquarters. Aunt Violet had called first to ascertain that Captain Tomas would not be there.

All around the huge complex police officers were coming and going. It was the hour for shift changes—a perfect time for Joe and Frank to get in and out without being noticed.

Their disguises didn't hurt, either. They were dressed in the brown uniforms of maintenance workers, which they'd bought at a uniform supply store on Canal Street. They also wore visored caps, which partially hid their faces, and black-framed glasses from the drugstore.

While Joe stood guard at the end of the second-floor hallway with a broom in his hands, Frank pulled a huge plastic garbage bag out of his pocket, and began going from office to office, emptying the contents of the trash cans.

After a few moments Frank stepped into Tomas's office and silently closed the door behind him. Looking into desk drawers, file cabinets, and the closet, he found nothing else to fuel his suspicions. He turned to the photo on the wall by the door and was just reaching for it when he heard Joe whistle. Frank stepped back and grabbed the wastebasket just as the door opened.

A uniformed sergeant appeared in the doorway. "Hey, fella! You new here?" he asked. "Don't believe we've met."

Looking up, Frank recognized the man as one

of the officers who had guarded them in the lockup.

"Name's Felix," Frank said, using his best Southern accent. "Just got hired."

The sergeant took him in for a long moment. "Listen," he finally said, "someone just broke a coffeepot in the squad room. Hustle down and clean it up, huh?"

"Sure thing, Sarge," Frank said, hoping the man wouldn't wait around until he complied. Luckily, the officer turned and left, his heels squeaking on the tile.

Not wasting another second, Frank took the photo off the wall, threw it into his garbage bag, and left the office. "Let's get out of here," he told Joe.

While Frank drove them home, Joe examined the photograph. "I can't believe this!" he said excitedly. "It's the same cabin! There's that old store down at the end of the dirt road—I remember noticing."

"Do you realize what this means, Joe?" Frank asked soberly.

"That Tomas and Billy were involved with each other somehow," Joe replied.

"I'm saying more than that," Frank said. "They both may have been mixed up with Stolarz's weapons smuggling scheme."

"But Tomas is a cop," Joe protested.

"Exactly. I hate to think it as much as you do,

but some cops are bad. And if Tomas is a part of it, it explains an awful lot. Like why he wouldn't tell us the reason Billy was under surveillance."

Joe's eyes lit up. "Maybe there *was* no surveillance! Maybe Tomas just said that to throw us off the track!"

"There are a lot of *maybes,*" Frank agreed. "One thing's for sure, though—we've got to go back out to that cabin. If we can find even the smallest shred of evidence to link Tomas to the scheme, we might be able to go over his head to higher-ups in the NOPD. Then maybe we can blow this whole thing wide open before any more illegal weapons get shipped to foreign customers!"

"We've got to try," Frank agreed. "If Tomas is involved in this thing, it won't be long before he tries to arrest us again. He's got to notice the photo is missing."

When they got back to Aunt Violet's, the Hardys gathered the others in the parlor and filled them in.

"That's awful!" Violet said, her cheeks reddening with anger. "Wait till I tell Chief Nolan that one of his top men is a criminal."

"Whoa, now," Frank cautioned. "I wouldn't say anything yet. Not until we confirm our suspicions. Violet, have you got a magnifying glass?"

"Sure do. Catlin, look in the drawer of the sideboard over there," Violet instructed.

Catlin quickly brought the magnifying glass over and gave it to Frank. He held it close to the photo, trying to make out the sign hanging over the old store in the background. " 'Skip's Hot Spot.' If we can find that, we can find the cabin."

Suddenly they heard sirens approaching from the direction of St. Charles Avenue. "The police are coming!" Vanessa cried, staring out the front window.

"We've got to get out of here fast!" Frank said.

Joe was already on his feet. Through the lace curtains at the front windows, he could see three cruisers pulling to a halt in front of the house. "I hate to run from the law," he said, "but we've got no choice."

"We'll call you first chance we get," Frank told the others. "Don't worry—it'll be okay." He swallowed hard, wishing he felt as positive as he was acting. "Try to stall them as long as you can. We'll need the head start."

Joe followed Frank to the rear of the house and out the back door. They climbed the high backyard fence to the roof of the neighboring garage, then jumped, tucking their heads and rolling when they hit the dirt of the driveway.

Almost in unison, they scrambled to their feet and ran like mad for the street.

Chapter

14

THEY RACED THROUGH BACKYARDS and down driveways, leaping fences when they had to, avoiding the busier streets of the Garden District.

"I think we made it," Joe gasped as he came to a stop at a large oak. He leaned against the trunk with both his hands held high over his head.

"Uh-huh," Frank agreed, unable to say anything else. He lay down on the grass that bordered the quiet side street where they'd finally stopped running, and didn't get up for about five minutes. By then, Joe, too, seemed to have recovered.

"Let's go someplace where we can talk this over."

Joe let go of the tree and stood up, looking at the street ahead of them. "Maybe there's someplace open down by that next traffic light," he said.

They found a run-down diner not far away, and after wolfing down some burgers and fries they decided it would be safe to call Aunt Violet's house.

Catlin answered the phone. "Thank goodness you're all right!" she said. "The police are gone now, but I'm sure they're looking for you. And they've got somebody watching the house, too."

"Great," Frank said disgustedly. "Listen, Catlin—can you drive your car to the corner of Sugarland and DeSoto and leave it for us? The police will be looking for our car."

"But won't the guy outside follow me?"

"Not if he's there to guard the house," Frank told her.

"Where exactly do I leave the car?"

"There's a parking lot next to an old diner at the corner," Frank explained. "Leave it there, with the keys under the seat and a good map in the glove compartment."

"Gotcha," Catlin said. "Good luck, Frank. We'll all be rootin' for you."

An hour later Frank and Joe were headed for bayou country. After a few wrong turns and several miles over rutted dirt roads, the brothers finally found the old store they'd seen in the photograph.

The place was boarded up and clearly deserted. Joe compared it with the photo he held in his hands. "This is the place," he said, "because there's the cabin we were at yesterday."

They drove Catlin's car about halfway down the dirt road and parked it in the shade before walking toward the cabin.

"I don't know what we think we're going to find here," Frank muttered. "It sure was empty yesterday."

Joe shook his head stubbornly. "It's too much of a coincidence, Frank. This place was on Billy Barta's navigational chart and now it's in Tomas's photograph."

"That doesn't *necessarily* mean Tomas is in on Stolarz's smuggling," Frank said.

Joe's jaw tightened. "What about that flash memory card?" he challenged Frank. "Sure, Stolarz could have pulled a switch, but it's more likely Tomas did it himself. And if you think about it, his investigation sure hasn't turned up much."

"True."

"He must have been thrilled to have a patsy like me to pin Billy's murder on," Joe said.

"Well, he did find you in Barta's apartment with the body on the floor next to you," Frank pointed out.

"And another thing," Joe said. "Tomas claims he had Billy under surveillance, but he won't tell us for what. It's possible that the reason Tomas was there that night is because he'd just killed Billy himself!"

"Joe," Frank said, "cool it. Tomas is a captain in the department. We can at least give him the benefit of the doubt."

They went inside. It was hot and sticky. The place smelled of fish and looked just as bare as it had the day before—with only one difference. One of the floorboards had been pried up. Next to it lay an open, empty metal box—smaller than the one that Frank had seen on the Elvis float, but the same kind. Frank bent down to examine it. The key that had opened the box was still in the lock. But the box was empty.

"We're too late," Frank said, disappointed. "Somebody's been here since we left."

"What do you think was in the box?"

Frank looked up at his brother. "If you ask me," he said, "I think it was the missing piece of computer hardware Stolarz was looking for—the interface that connected the software to the missile. The part Redfern told Stolarz he had when they argued that night. What do you think?"

The answer to Frank's question came not from Joe, but from an eerily familiar voice behind them. "Very good, Mr. Hardy. Only it wasn't Redfern that night—it was *me!*"

Frank and Joe spun around and found themselves staring into the steely eyes of Captain Tomas. He had an automatic pistol pointed right at them.

"You fellas are much better than I gave you credit for," Tomas said grimly, kicking the cabin door shut without taking his eyes off the brothers. "I underestimated you. But I won't make that mistake again. Have a seat," he said, indicating the two rickety wooden chairs that sat in the middle of the cabin. "Go on, sit down. *Slowly.*"

"I guess you heard everything we said," Frank said.

"Just about," Tomas responded. "I've been out here waitin' for you. When I came into my office and saw the photograph gone, I figured you'd swiped it. So I sent my men over to where you were stayin', but you were gone. Didn't take much to figure out where you were headed."

"Who threw that grenade yesterday?" Frank asked.

"Redfern," Tomas said, a trace of weariness coming into his voice. "I told Stolarz you fellas were onto him, and he set his goon on you."

"So it was *you* that night at Redfern's apartment, arguing with Stolarz," Frank said.

"Yep, that was me," Tomas said, pulling some heavy plastic strips out of his pocket—disposable police handcuffs, with one-way latches on the ends.

"That car we heard pulling up in the street—" Joe began.

"Mine," Tomas cut him off. "Redfern got in, I put on his coat and hat, and I went inside. Got to take extraordinary precautions when you're in my position."

"So let me get this straight," Frank said. "You and Stolarz were partners—"

"No, that's not the way it was—at least not in the beginning," Tomas said. "Sorry, but you fellas will have to oblige me by lettin' me tie you up. I can't have you movin' around while I'm cashin' in on all my hard work."

Methodically, he tied their arms behind their backs, and their legs to the legs of the chairs. When they were bound fast, Tomas leaned back against the wall by the door and glanced at his watch.

"So you weren't partners at first?" Frank pressed, sensing that Tomas wasn't going to let this go on much longer.

"Look," Tomas said, with a sigh of weariness. "For fifteen years I was a good cop—one o' the best on the force. And all those years, I had my eye set on chief of detectives. I figure I work hard, earn that promotion, I get out in twenty years with a nice fat pension. But things don't work that way in real life, y'see. It's all politics— who you know, not what you do. I took big chances to get that promotion. And I got shot instead. Right in the face."

He traced a finger down the long scar on his forehead. "Spent six months in bed, and by the time I got back, a lot o' bootlickin' pencil pushers had gone up the ladder ahead of me." He examined his gun carefully. "That's when I decided that bein' a good cop wasn't ever goin' to pay. On the other hand, crime *does* pay—big time. And right about then, I stumbled onto Barta and Stolarz, and their little smugglin' gig."

"How did you find out about it?" Frank asked. He quietly worked to free his wrists, but the plastic cords held fast.

"Antoine LeMieux," Tomas explained. "Nice kid, that Antoine. I knew him from fishin' on Pontchartrain, and he invited me into this Mardi Gras krewe they had—Xanadu, it was called. Billy was in it, and they stored their floats at Stolarz's warehouse. That's how I came to find out what they were up to. I got an eye for dirty doin's after fifteen years on the force. So it didn't take me long to convince Billy to hand me a piece of the action."

"And you killed Antoine?" Joe asked, his voice full of bitterness.

Tomas shook his head. "No, no," he said. "I wouldn'a done that. Like I told you, Antoine was a nice fella. I was just meetin' up with Billy on the lake one night on our way out to the Gulf.

He and Antoine were havin' a fight over somethin', I don't know what. He punched Antoine, and Antoine fell into the lake. Propellers got him—chewed him right up. Sad . . ." He sighed again, and then checked his watch. "Look, I got to get goin'—"

"Wait!" Frank stopped him. "What about Billy? What happened next?"

"All right," Tomas said. "I suppose I owe you an explanation." He wiped the sweat off his forehead with his sleeve and smiled wryly. "Once I got in on things, it was the three of us—me, Stolarz, and Billy. Except me and Billy were only goin' to get ten percent each. Stolarz thought—still thinks—that just 'cause he set the business up, he deserves most of the money. Well, I didn't like that much. There was a big fat pie, and I wasn't satisfied with a small piece of it. I mean, I'd already betrayed my badge. I figured I might as well make it pay. So I talked Billy into stealin' the interface and makin' Stolarz split everything three ways in exchange for gettin' it back."

"What went wrong?" Frank asked.

Tomas sighed again. "Seems Billy didn't like me pushin' him around. He threatened me—said he was gonna tell Stolarz what we'd done, and blame it all on me. Well, now, you can see why I had to kill him, can't you? I don't like bein' fooled with like that. No, indeed. I'm used to holdin' all the cards. Just like I do right now."

He rubbed a hand along the barrel of his gun. "I hit him on the head with my billy club. I didn't think he'd bleed like that—I had to go clean the club up. I left the door open and the music on, and took his backpack, to make it look like a robbery. Too bad you had to walk in on things like you did, Joe. It made a real mess out of everything. You see, I had me a suspect, and I had to take advantage. Only I didn't figure you and your brother to be detectives. The NOPD could really have used you two."

"What about Stolarz?" Joe asked.

Tomas frowned. "Thought he could treat me like a rent-a-cop. But I straightened him out. Told him it had to be fifty-fifty now that Billy's gone, 'cause I had the interface he needed to complete the deal. I see where Redfern went lookin' for it here after he tried to blow you boys up," he added, looking at the floorboard and the empty strongbox. "Luckily, I'd already been here and taken it out. It's on my boat now—right down the bayou."

He pulled a pack of wooden matches out of his pocket and shook it absentmindedly. "See, y'all didn't realize it, but it was me you were tryin' to catch ever since that first day. I bounced you off the streetcar, Joe, and you've never caught up with me since then. I cleaned out Billy's desk and his apartment, just in case he had anything to implicate me. I gave you a blank flash memory card, and kept the one you gave me . . . like I said, you never had a chance."

"Now what?" Frank asked, feeling beads of sweat begin to trickle down his face.

"I'm going to deliver my piece of this deal, collect my reward, and sail off into the sunset, a rich man," Tomas said, turning back to Frank. "Stolarz will finally be able to make his delivery to his clients, and I'll live happily ever after in Brazil or maybe Argentina—someplace where they know how to treat a man with money and aren't likely to send me back to the U.S. After all, it may get a little hot around here pretty soon."

He shook the pack of matches again and with a long, mournful sigh slowly opened the door of the cabin.

"It's been nice knowin' you fellas. Sorry it had to end like this." With a respectful nod of his head, he stepped through the door and slammed it shut behind him.

Frank glanced over at Joe, whose skin had gone ash gray. Frank knew he was probably the same color himself. He yanked frantically on his bonds, but they didn't give at all. And then he smelled it.

"Smoke!" Frank said, feeling the panic rising inside him. "Joe—he's set the cabin on fire!"

Chapter

15

NO SOONER HAD FRANK uttered the words than the entire front wall of the cabin burst into flames. Frank and Joe tried, but their bonds wouldn't budge. Even worse, the two chairs had been strapped to the table legs. There was no way they could fit through the doorway or window without getting free first.

"We've got to get out of here!" Joe said. Thick smoke was creeping toward them. Suddenly, Joe burst out laughing.

"Joe, are you okay?" Frank asked desperately. "You've got to hang in there. We'll come up with something."

"I just did!" Joe gasped. "That's what's so funny," he went on as he reached for his belt. It was the one Frank had given him for Christmas—the one with the little knife concealed in the buckle.

"I forgot all about that buckle," Frank said, coughing as the smoke grew thicker.

"So did I," Joe replied, painstakingly maneuvering his fingers so he could grab the belt, then pulling it around bit by bit until the buckle was behind his back. As soon as he could reach the buckle with his hands, he opened the little knife and started cutting his wrists free. "I told you when you gave it to me, I thought it was a ridiculous gadget."

"Ridiculous, huh?"

"Okay, okay, it saved our lives," Joe said, cutting Frank loose.

The smoke was so thick they were both coughing and gasping for air.

Frank took a running leap and dove through the single open window. Joe followed, and not a moment too soon. He hit the muddy ground, and kept rolling until he was submerged in the bayou. Just as he went under, the cabin exploded in a ball of flame, sending out a white-hot blast.

When Joe surfaced, he saw his brother standing in the shallow water next to him, staring at what was left of Tomas's cabin.

"That could have been us," Frank said.

Joe blew out a relieved breath. "Close," he

said. "Really close that time. Madame LeMieux strikes again."

"Never mind that. Let's get out of here," Frank said, climbing out. "Tomas took his boat, which is the short way to Stolarz's warehouse. We've got to go the long way—by road—and get there before they take off."

Minutes later the guys were back on the highway. When they reached the city, Joe slowed down. "I hate to say this," he said, "but I'm going to have to pull over for gas. This thing's flashing red on me."

"It's okay," Frank said. "I'll call Catlin while you're filling up. Maybe they can get us some help."

"Good thinking," Joe said. "But I don't think there's enough time for them to do anything. If we don't get down to the warehouse dock fast, all the evidence is going to be on a boat to someplace far away!"

Joe gassed up the car at a station near the waterfront. By the time he had paid the attendant, Frank was back. "Okay, let's get out of here," he said as he got in alongside Joe.

"What did Catlin say?" Joe asked.

"She said the police were at Violet's house again about an hour ago. They wanted the make and license number of Catlin's car."

"That's *this* car!" Joe groaned.

"So let's move it," Frank said grimly.

They pulled out into traffic again, but five blocks down the road, they heard a siren. Joe felt his heart start hammering. Peering into the rearview mirror, he saw a squad car about half a block behind them. "Do I pull over, or what?" Joe asked, panic in his voice.

"If we do, we blow our only chance to get Tomas."

Just then a voice sounded over a police bullhorn. "Pull over. Stop the car, and keep your hands in sight!"

Torn between his need to catch Tomas and his reluctance to disobey the order, Joe stopped the car before the next corner, and both he and Frank raised their hands. In the rearview mirror, Joe saw two burly officers get out of the squad car and come toward them, hands on their guns, which were still in their holsters.

Although he had stopped the car, Joe had not shifted into Park or shut off the engine. When the police were just a few feet short of the car, Joe lifted his foot off the brake and hit the accelerator hard. The tires burned rubber, sending a cloud of dust and smoke out behind them, which left the two officers coughing.

In seconds the Hardys were out in the intersection. Luckily, the light had just changed in their favor. Frank glanced back to see the men scrambling toward their squad car, shouting into their walkie-talkies as they ran.

"Whew!" Joe said as they raced down the street, police sirens wailing all around them now. "I really hated to do that. We're going to have a lot of explaining to do if we ever get out of this mess."

"There's the warehouse up ahead," Frank said, pointing. But just then another squad car screeched around a corner behind them. "Step on it, Joe!" Frank yelled.

"What do you think I've been doing all this time?" Joe shouted back, holding the steering wheel at arm's length as the car rattled over some potholes at breakneck speed.

"They're gaining on us," Frank said. "Quick, turn in here at the parking lot—there's no sense going through the front door. Tomas and Stolarz will be out back at the docks."

"The side door to the warehouse is open," Joe said, heading right for the door that led out to the parking lot. The brakes screeched as the car skidded to a halt.

Frank and Joe were out of the car and inside the warehouse before the cruiser reached the side door. The last thing Joe saw before he turned and ran for the dock was the two officers getting out and drawing their guns.

"Joe—the floats!" Frank said, pointing to the huge constructions that lined either side of the warehouse's center aisle. Joe and Frank proceeded to yank down whatever they could—a giant clown head, a huge but almost weightless fiberglass arm, the face of Snow White. They tossed the giant pieces into the aisle behind them, making an obstacle course for the police pursuing them.

Then they dashed to the loading dock doors. Joe threw them open.

There, below them on the wharf, were Ron Stolarz, Ralph Redfern, and Captain Tomas. Stolarz was clutching the metal strongbox to his chest, keeping it from Tomas's grasp. Ralph Redfern lay between the two, dead. Tomas held a smoking gun in his hand.

"Look!" Stolarz shouted, seeing the Hardys. "I thought you said you got rid of them!"

Tomas gasped. "I don't believe it!"

"Well, finish the job," Stolarz ordered. "We've got to get out of here right away. If you hadn't been so greedy, we'd have been long gone."

"Shut up!" Tomas ordered. Suddenly he waved the gun at the Hardys. "Fifty percent isn't greedy—and if Redfern hadn't made such a fuss about it, I wouldn't have had to kill him. As for these two," he added, leveling his gun at Frank, "they're history!"

Chapter

16

FRANK WAS WITHIN leaping distance of Tomas with the boat three steps below him, but it was too late now, and Frank knew it.

At that precise moment, though, the door on the side of the warehouse flew open. The two police who'd been chasing Frank and Joe appeared there. They stood still, out of breath and utterly confused by the sight in front of them. Tomas glanced up at them.

In the mere half second during which Tomas was distracted, Frank took a leap, landing on Tomas before he could get off a clean shot. The gun fired wildly into the air and went flying as Frank grabbed Tomas's right arm and slammed it onto a wooden piling.

Giving him no chance to recover, Frank lifted the crooked cop to his feet and delivered a flying kick to the midsection that sent Tomas over the edge of the wharf and into the water.

Frank saw Stolarz clambering onto the boat. He started the engine and cast off.

Joe leapt onto the boat at the last possible moment and yanked Stolarz's hands off the controls, causing the boat to come about and hit the dock. Joe quickly turned off the engine, then spun around to deal with Stolarz.

"All right, everybody freeze right where you are!" screamed the first of the two officers to recover his wits and scramble down the steps to the dock. He held his pistol in his hands and was waving it around nervously. His companion stood behind him, also with his pistol drawn.

"What's this all about, Captain Tomas?" the first officer asked, helping his superior out of the water.

"Glad you got here in time, Sergeant Dooley," Tomas said, shaking himself off. "These two kids are dangerous."

"He's the dangerous one!" Joe shouted, pointing at Tomas. "He and his friend—they were about to smuggle sensitive weapons technology out of the country!"

Tomas laughed as if it were totally preposterous. Stolarz, taking his cue, started laughing along with him.

"You know me, boys," Tomas said. "How long have we been on the force together? Ten years? And you know Mr. Stolarz. These two kids are the ones who were doing the smugglin'. I caught up to 'em just before you got here."

"That's funny," said the first officer. " 'Cause we were chasin' 'em, too. They only got here a few seconds ago."

"Right," Tomas corrected himself. "I was waitin' for 'em—lured 'em here, into a trap."

"He's full of baloney," Joe insisted. "Can't you see? Look at that strongbox loaded with computer boards and flash memory cards. You saw for yourselves that Stolarz was carrying it. And neither Frank nor I have a weapon—but I'll bet if you search Stolarz's boat, you'll find some heavy firepower."

The officer named Dooley looked at his companion. "What do you think, Jack?" he asked, picking up Tomas's revolver and considering whether or not to hand it back to its owner.

"Beats me," Jack answered. "But I'd hate to drag the captain and Mr. Stolarz downtown in cuffs and be wrong about it, wouldn't you?"

Just then a police siren split the air. Moments later, two squad cars turned into the parking lot and screeched to a halt along the dock.

A man in full dress uniform, accompanied by several lieutenants, stepped out of the first one.

"Chief Nolan!" Officer Dooley exclaimed, saluting.

Catlin, Vanessa, Aunt Violet, and All-Night Al piled out of the second car.

"What in blazes is going on here?" Chief Nolan barked, striding over to where Ralph Redfern lay sprawled on the wharf. "What are you two men doing?" he asked Dooley and his partner.

"They were just about to take these two kids in for murder," Tomas answered for them. "Weren't you, boys?"

"We . . . uh . . ." Dooley hesitated.

"Chief Nolan," Frank broke in. "Captain Tomas and Mr. Stolarz were about to deliver advanced missile targeting systems to a foreign government."

"What?" The chief stared at Frank as if he'd just told him that Martians had landed in New Orleans.

"Don't buy any of his garbage," Tomas called out. "I've been onto these kids from the beginning. I was just springing the trap on them when these officers showed up!"

"He's right, Chief Nolan," Stolarz said. "Captain Tomas asked me to help him reel in these smugglers."

"Now I don't know who to believe!" the chief said, removing his hat and wiping the sweat from his brow.

"Chief," Frank said, "if you want proof, all you have to do is search Stolarz's boat—the computer boards and flash memory cards are in that metal strongbox on the deck."

Stolarz and Tomas exchanged worried glances. Joe noticed it, and so did the chief. "What about that, Tomas?" he asked.

"We'd just taken the stuff from those two, Chief," Tomas explained.

"Check the prints on the strongbox—and on that gun, too, if you don't believe us," Joe said, pointing to Tomas's automatic pistol. "It's Tomas's—he'd just killed Mr. Redfern when we got here."

"Take that gun as evidence," the chief instructed one of the officers who'd accompanied him. "In the meantime let's haul the whole lot of them down to headquarters, and search the boat for weapons and contraband."

Then the chief turned to Tomas. "If you're innocent, you've got nothing to worry about. But if your prints are on that gun, you've got a lot of explaining to do."

A few hours later it was all over. The fingerprints and ballistics tests confirmed what the Hardys had already told the chief. Stolarz confessed to weapons smuggling, and agreed to testify against Captain Tomas in return for leniency—although he wouldn't get much. Tomas was booked for conspiracy, weapons smuggling, and two counts of murder.

That night Frank, Joe, Catlin, Vanessa, Violet, and All-Night Al sat at a table in the backyard garden of Brennan's, one of New Orleans's landmark restaurants. They all had heaping servings of gumbo—in Al's case, his second of the evening.

"Al," Joe said, "you're the only guy I've ever seen who could give me a run for my money in the appetite department!"

"Isn't he the sweetest boy you ever met?" Violet asked Al, giving Joe an affectionate hug.

"Sweet ain't the word," Al said with a laugh. "Him and his brother been turnin' my hair gray all week."

"Now, Al," Violet chided him. "At least they brought you and me back together."

"Why, Violet," Al said, putting down his fork for the first time since the food had arrived.

"I detect romance in the air," Catlin said, giving Vanessa a wink.

"Oh, stop," Violet told her. "Everybody just eat up."

"By the way, guys, have you called your parents yet?" Catlin asked the Hardys.

"Uh-huh," Joe answered. "Mom was pretty upset when we told her how much trouble we'd been in."

"Yeah," Frank concurred. "But we talked her

into letting us stay down here a few extra days. That is, if it's okay with you, Aunt Violet."

"Why, I'd be thrilled to have you!" Violet said.

"You've been great to us," Frank said sincerely. "You, too, Al. Without you, we'd probably be behind bars."

Joe shook his head sadly. "I still can't believe Captain Tomas is a murderer. It makes me sick that a police officer could turn so bad."

"It happens," Al said, sighing. "Not too often, mind you. But when a good cop does go bad, ain't nothin' worse."

Joe pushed his plate away, leaned back in his chair, and stared up at the sky. It was full of bright, twinkling stars. "Hey, you guys," he said. "How do you suppose Madame LeMieux did it? I mean, she predicted everything that happened."

"Oh, brother," Frank said. "Here we go again. I told you, Joe—those predictions were vague enough so that no matter what happened, something about them was bound to sound right."

Joe shook his head. "You'll never convince me of that." He reached into his pocket for a paperback he'd bought at a bookstore in the French Quarter just an hour ago. "In fact, I've decided to take up fortune-telling myself!"

Frank read the book's title, and raised a skeptical eyebrow. " *'Tarot and You'?*" he said. "Oh, boy. This is just great. Joe, how about we just enjoy tonight, and let the future take care of itself? After all, there are some things it's better not to know in advance."

"Okay," Joe said with a shrug as he put the book back in his jacket pocket. "But whenever you're ready, remember—Monsieur Hardy knows all."

Frank and Joe's next case:

Oliver Richards writes action-adventure novels, and he wants to make Frank and Joe the stars of his next thriller. But he's unwittingly drawn them into a real-life tale of intrigue and danger. Thanks to him, the Assassins—an infamous international gang of professional killers—are back, and the Hardys are at the top of their hit list! In their long and deadly war against the Assassins, the boys have always relied on the Gray Man, top operative in an ultrasecret government agency. But now he may have turned traitor, and they don't know whom to trust. One thing they know for sure: the terrorists are cold and ruthless ... and their latest evil scheme could put seven million lives at risk ... in *True Thriller*, Case #100 in The Hardy Boys Casefiles™.